ROOM NUMBER 8

ROOM NUMBER 8

YAHYA KHAN

Translated from Arabic by
Heba Nafez Thabet

ROOM NUMBER 8
Yahya Khan

Published by Nomad Publishing in 2023
Email: info@nomad-publishing.com
www.nomad-publishing.com

ISBN 9781914325458

© Yahya Khan 2023

 The Publishers would like
to thank the Harf Literary Agency

Disclaimer: The content and any opinions included in such content reflect the views and opinions of the author and do not reflect the opinions and beliefs of the publisher, the translator, Tarjim program, or any of their affiliates. The author is solely responsible for any statements made in such content and any translation is made based on the perception of the author from the original language or source of information prior to any translation or adaptation made.

Contents

Part I
The Horror on the Ground Floor — 15

Part II
The Room and
the Human Time Bomb — 41

Part III
The War Within — 189

Part IV
The Difficult Return — 223

*In the name of God, the Merciful and
the Compassionate
Prayer and peace be upon the most honourable
Prophet Mohammed, his family, and all his
companions …*

*May God assist me in presenting this book
in a way that pleases You.
Without your help, such a success could have never
been achieved", and without Your blessing,
the reward of good deeds would have
never been attained.*

Yahya Khan

Dedication

To my father and mother,

to whom I dedicate what I have achieved in my life.

To my wife,

whose support and encouragement

whilst I write are the keys to success.

To my children,

whose presence in my life has enriched it.

Opening Whisper

This novel is based on real events that took place in a hostel.

PART I
THE HORROR ON THE GROUND FLOOR

Makkah 1992

Chapter 1

A cold shiver penetrated his body, and his heart started racing, as cold shiver penetrated his body, and his heart started racing, as he stood silently.

He often had the same feeling in the same place, which was the ground-floor entrance to his family's house. The entrance led to a small antechamber with a single door to the main floor and, opposite it, a stairway to the upper floor. His parents had designated the ground floor as the space, in which they hosted visitors on formal occasions, but since most of their relatives lived in Jeddah and his family was relatively small, they only occupied the upper floor; the door to the main one stayed shut between visits by any guests.

Each time he came or went, the same question hung in the air, "Why do I feel uneasy whenever I get closer to this particular spot?"

The final exams for his last term in secondary school were approaching, so he decided to go down to the ground floor every day, away from the noise and distraction caused by his younger brother, which would help him to focus on his homework, revisions, and studying. He requested his parents and they gave him the permission.

Despite finding the quietness he had been seeking, he also experienced strange feelings, whenever he used that space. He would start to feel agitated and confused, even frenetic, and a disturbing blend of sensations often assaulted him out of the blue as he was trying to focus on his lessons. It usually lasted for a few minutes, then vanished, only to return after a while. He would keep struggling with that troubling feeling until finishing his studies for the day and joining his family on the upper floor.

He was only seventeen, too young to understand the feelings he was having, or even to seek help interpreting his strange emotions. Mainly, he did not want to ask his parents, because he was not sure.

Right now, he was standing in the antechamber, staring at the door, trying to decide whether he should go upstairs and not enter the ground floor, or just go in and try to work around his negative feelings for the coming hours, as he had in the previous days.

He took a deep breath and whispered saying,"In the name of God, the Merciful the Compassionate. Then, he grabbed the doorknob, and turned it quickly, before his courage could evaporate.

Then, he went upstairs instead.

Chapter 2

Total darkness.

That is what he always encountered, whenever he entered the place. So, his left hand spontaneously went to the switch on the wall, knowing the comfort of light would shield him from the gloom of the blackness.

But this time was different. With the first flash of the light, he thought he saw someone – or something – dashing quickly to hide behind one of the internal partitions that divided the rooms. The young man was startled. Holding his breath for a few seconds, he tried to listen for any strange sound but heard nothing. The place sank into an irritating silence.

He breathed out restlessly, blaming himself for his unjustified fear. He knew quite well that the other door leading to the outer courtyard, was firmly locked and was never opened unless guests were coming. The windows were tightly shut, too, and all this confirmed that no one was there; his mother and brother were upstairs, and his father was out, as usual, working his job as a real estate agent or buying stuff for the family.

The young man stepped forward, quietly closing the door behind him. He turned right into one of the guest rooms, the one that held a rectangular wooden table in addition to its fine furniture. His father had bought him that table a few months ago because it suited the requirements for architectural drawings and the various items needed to make them, including the long T-square ruler. As usual, he switched on the air conditioner, more to let its monotone hum dispel some of the gloominess than to chill the place, which tended to remain cool throughout the year.

He was soon engrossed in his studies, doing homework assignments and revising his lessons, until those mysterious goose-bumps returned. To him it felt like whatever caused that feeling was saying, "I did not forget you today, just arrived late to manipulate your mood!" He started to turn, right and left and all around him, looking for anything that might explain the way he felt. He had a feeling that he was being watched, but he cast that thought aside at once for how silly it was.

He then busied himself by looking into the next homework assignment and retrieving … the necessary drawing tools out of their box. Another hour passed before his body suddenly trembled and his heart shook inside his chest. The shudder overwhelmed him, shook him hard, and something else also happened at that moment, something creepy and mysterious.

Chapter 3

The young man's father parked the family car by the pavement opposite their house, the same spot where he parked every day, and got out holding an open-topped box containing all the shopping his wife had written on her list.

He passed through the iron outer gate to the property and walked slowly across the courtyard. Seeing light coming from the ground floor, he realized that his son was there, studying in the room he had prepared for that reason. He said a quick prayer for him and continued on his way, heading towards the smaller iron door that led to the interior stairs.

Chapter 4

It was a noise. And not just any noise. It was a substantial one that had no business being heard because that part of the house was supposed to be – had to be – empty.

That was what had disturbed the young man and provoked his anxiety. The noise was strong and had a metallic resonance, echoing off the walls of the ground floor for some moments before silence once again prevailed over the place, except for one spot: the young man's mind. He stood suddenly and, questions swirling around inside his head, moved hesitantly out of the room and into the wide hall that ran between the guest rooms. His gaze soon fell on the source of the noise.

There, on the floor in one of the corners of the hall, lay one of the numerous brass antiques that filled the ground level. It had come apart into three pieces. The young man exhaled impatiently as he walked towards it, then said to himself out loud, "I don't understand why my parents still keep these antiques after all these years. I can't wait for the day we get rid of them."

He put the pieces back together quickly, silently wondering how the object had fallen from its long stand. He placed the reassembled antique back on the stand, then checked carefully to make sure it was secure. He was about to release his grasp when he sensed it: someone watching him over his shoulder! His imagination raced, trying to discern who could possibly be standing behind him, and he whirled around as quickly as he could to face the danger. And there stood ... no one. He was quite alone in the hall.

His eyebrows came together in a tight furrow, anxiety and distress turning instantly to rage at the mystery that always surrounded the place. He looked all around again in an attempt to figure out what had happened. Finding no answers, he called out to the void, "What on earth is happening here? Is anybody here?"

It was a rhetorical question, so he expected no reply, which is why he gasped in terror when a voice answered, "I'm here."

Chapter 5

"Dad!"

The word came out loudly. The young man had turned his whole body towards the voice, ready to confront whoever had answered him, only to find his own father standing there. He was in the doorway at the beginning of the hall, his hand still holding the knob on the open door.

"Yes, it's me, my son. I was about to go upstairs when I heard you shouting, but I couldn't make out what you were saying until I opened the door."

The son felt greatly ashamed by what had happened, so he rubbed the back of his head and avoided direct eye contact. "I'm sorry about that Dad," he said. "I guess exam season has made me a little jumpy."

The man pondered his son's expression for a few seconds, gauging his son's status and wondering if he was withholding something. Then he spoke.

"That's okay. Do your best, son, and put your trust in God."

"Yes, by God."

"It's getting late. Try to finish up as soon as you can, and may God grant you success."

The father left and closed the door behind him before he could see his son nodding his head at him. When silence had settled over the hall again, the young man started laughing at the silly "scenario" that he had just faced.

Suddenly, the laugh stopped in his throat and what

escaped from between his lips was a quick grunt as he felt a heavy blow to his face. His eyes widened at this even more peculiar situation. It was as if some invisible person had struck him with such a hard punch that his whole body had been pushed back a few steps.

For a moment, his senses seemed to have malfunctioned. He could see nothing but whiteness surrounding him in all directions, and all he could hear was a buzz. He also felt pain all over his body, so severely that it prevented him from breathing. It was just for a few seconds, but it felt like an age to him. *Was that how it feels to face death?* Soon the pain disappeared, his vision and hearing came back, and the buzz went silent. Everything suddenly vanished into the same thin air from which it had so quickly emerged.

Except for the question: *Was that how it feels to face death?* That stayed with him for quite awhile.

Chapter 6

As he lay in bed on his back that night, he closed his eyes and tried to clear his thoughts. His mind needed free rein if he were figure out the events he had experienced downstairs a few hours earlier. How strange it was that something which took no more than a few moments could defy explanation. He was deeply puzzled, and would have concluded that what he remembered was simply not possible – were it not for the pain and itchiness in a certain spot under his chin.

He raised his hand to that spot and pressed it with his fingers, trying to understand the nature of what he was feeling. The pain had already started to recede, but it was still there. And that was not all. There was something else that disturbed him, too, an intangible but unmistakable feeling that something had changed inside him: he was not the same as before.

At that moment, he really wished his older brother were there on the bed next to his, so he could share what had happened with him, and together they could try to reach some sort of logical explanation.

He opened his eyes with his head turned to the right to look at the empty bed. It had been like that for two years, ever since his brother had enrolled at one of the Eastern Province universities which had become very popular because its high academic ranking somewhat ensured – with God's will – that its graduates would find employment with the best companies.

ROOM NUMBER 8

He returned his head to its prior position and closed his eyes, thinking about his own future. He was determined to join the same university, since it was the best in its category, as everyone insisted. He strived for the best and would settle for nothing less.

Eventually the young man slept deeply, and much of the night had passed before he woke up shivering from the cold. He soon discovered that the blanket in which he had wrapped himself seemed to have shrunk, so that it no longer covered most of his body. That had never happened before. He shifted his weight onto his right arm, using it to raise his upper body off the bed so his other hand could reach the edge of the blanket and pull it over him again.

As soon as his head touched the pillow again, a new wave of pain struck him under the chin, instantly followed by a severe headache. He gasped as the surprise, then bit his lower lip and held his head in his hands, hoping to relieve the pain and avoid making any more noise that might wake his little brother, who, he now realized, lay sleeping on the bed beside him. He felt overwhelmed by anxiety and disturbance.

The headache went away just as quickly as it had come on, and the pain under his chin eased, too, so he stopped biting his lip and released a few deep sighs. He had only one question in his mind: *Is it normal for those kinds of pains to strike so suddenly and then disappear within a single minute?*

He soon got his answer, but in a peculiar – and horrifying – way.

Chapter 7

"Is something bothering you?"

The wife's whispered question came after her husband had spent some time pacing the bedroom with his hands clasped behind his back. The light was too dim to see his features clearly, but she could hear the deep breath that issued from his chest, followed by a brief reply:

"The ground floor."

The wife sat up straighter on the bed, and an anxious tone crept into her voice with her next question.

"The ground floor! Is there anything new about it?"

"I'm not sure. I might be wrong in my thinking ... but ... maybe it's starting to affect our son!"

She covered her face with her hands. That piece of information drove up her heart rate. Ever since her husband had bought the house a year earlier, he had begun to have strange, disturbing dreams that were always connected to the ground floor, and both of them had been infused with even weirder sensations whenever they entered that part of the house alone.

"That's really concerning," she said, "but maybe he hasn't felt anything. Could it be that it was just you who felt something?"

"Perhaps, but I prefer not to ask him any explicit questions about it."

"How would we know if he was really suffering from

something related to the ground floor?"

"Only God Almighty knows. All we can do is to watch our son closely in the coming days, but taking care not to worry him or make him feel anxious."

She nodded her head in consent before adding, "with our sincerest prayers for God to protect him from any harm."

Chapter 8

Back in his room, their astonished son was wondering about the nature of what he had been going through when he was startled yet again, this time by a bizarre feminine voice that made his blood run cold.

He flinched hard when he received the words: "Our world is full of mysteries and our abilities are beyond what your small mind can imagine, human. Those quick pains in your body are just one example."

It sounded like the hissing of a snake, and the young man was sure that he had heard it from inside his own head rather than through his ears.

He tried to search for the source of the voice, but quickly realized that he couldn't move his head – or any other part of his body. He was effectively paralyzed, and the realization filled his entire being with terror. Emotions wrestled inside his head, but despite great difficulty, he managed to speak out in a very weak voice:

"In the name of God, the most Merciful, the most Compassionate. Dear God, what is happening to me?"

He felt pressure inside his head as the angry voice returned.

"I did not expect you to be that weak," it said. "Stop saying these words."

He felt the urge to cry and his vocal cords produced a faint whine that slipped past his lips before he managed to ask: "Who are you? And what is this paralysis in my body?"

"I told you that we had great powers. Don't you know about demons, genies, and goblins, you nasty human?"

He could feel that his pulse was off the charts. He tried to concentrate and form an answer, but panic had dulled his wits. He answered nonetheless, albeit anxiously, "Demons and genies? I seek refuge in God from Satan. I seek refuge in God ... Get away from me. You're nothing but a painful nightmare, a nightmare!"

"Now you return to using the forbidden words ... May you be screwed with the curse of the demons' kings, you fool!"

She had screamed the last sentence, increasing the pain and pressure inside his head until he thought his mind itself would certainly explode.

And then it was over. The headache completely vanished and the young man regained control over his body. He still struggled to take a breath, however, so he sat up straight in his bed and tried to take stock of the terror and suffering he had just experienced.

With each passing moment, he regained a little more of his composure. He had felt chills to the bone when that voice was assailing him, but now he used tissue paper to mop up the sweat that had drenched his hair and run down his face. He covered his face with his hands, releasing a long sigh and a whispered prayer:

"I seek refuge in God from Satan. I seek refuge in God."

Chapter 9

Here he was. It was early evening on the day after the horrifying night before, and the young man stood before the door to the ground floor, schoolbag in hand. He was quite exhausted, as he had not been able to sleep after the terror of the previous night. The fatigue had been evident on his face since the morning, and all of his classmates and teachers had noticed his pallor. One close friend had even pressed him about it, saying he felt something different about him, something beyond his pale face. The young man tried hard to dispel such notions from his friend's mind, even though they mirrored precisely what he himself had been thinking since the inexplicable blow to the face he had suffered the previous day.

And now he faced a difficult decision. Should he turn around and scrap the idea of ever coming down to the ground floor again, or should he challenge everything, cross the doorway, and head into the unknown? Did he have enough courage to enter that space again after all that had happened?

For some unknown reason, one that defied his own expectations and drove his heart rate skyward, he found himself turning the knob, pushing the door open, and taking a few steps inside. He reached for the light switch, prepared himself to catch any movement that might take place when the lights came on, and flipped the switch into the "ON" position.

Nothing. Darkness remained the master of the ground floor.

He flipped the switch several times, but got the same result each time: the lights refused to deliver. Wearily, he pursed his lips and wondered if this was just a coincidence or if it was somehow connected to everything that had happened the day – and night – before.

Moments later, he thought he heard a noise coming from somewhere on the ground floor, and a shudder ran through his body. He withdrew immediately, closed the door tightly behind him, and rushed up the inner staircase.

"Why did you come back up here? You're not going to study downstairs?"

That was how his mother reacted when he got upstairs. She looked both surprised and inquisitive.

"No, I'm not," he answered with a shake of his head. "The lights aren't working."

"Not working? Are you sure?"

"Yes, I'm sure, Mum," he said. "Please ask Dad to call an electrician tomorrow to check everything: the switches, the wiring, and the bulbs."

"I'll tell him for sure, but tomorrow is Wednesday, and in the evening we'll be going to Jeddah to spend the weekend at my parents' house."

Her son's features lit up with enthusiasm.

"Oh my God! How could I have forgotten?" he exclaimed. "I wait for that visit every month. Spending two days with my uncle and my cousins is such an irreplaceable pleasure. It seems that being immersed in my studies has made me forgetful."

His mother gave him a wide, encouraging smile, followed by her prayers: "May God assist you, my son. I ask Him to pave the way for you and your brothers and grant you success in your lives."

Chapter 10

That night, the young man was determined to stay awake for fear of repeating the nightmare, but the mental and physical fatigue defeated his resistance and pulled him into the world dreams. He found himself standing, half-naked, atop a snow-capped mountain, the bitter cold whipping his limbs without remorse.

He was aware that it was a dream, and it was the kind in which the dreamer sees himself amidst unfolding events. If the dream is pleasant, the dreamer can will it to continue, allowing him to sink more deeply into it. But if such dreams carry pain or distress, like this one, he can often get out of it by waking up.

When he finally was able to open his eyes, he saw the ceiling of his own room and let out a sigh of relief. Even though he was off the snowy mountaintop, however, he still felt cold. He quickly realized why. The blanket had not just shrunk a bit like the previous night: rather, it was in a pile on the floor beside the bed!

In an instant, the storms of horror and disturbance were battering his mind and his soul once again. The pain under his chin was back, as was the terrifying paralysis.

"We meet again, human."

It was the same malevolent female voice, and just like before, it hissed the words at him from inside his head. He struggled mightily to activate the muscles of his body, but it was no use.

ROOM NUMBER 8

"You are either very stubborn or very stupid," the voice sneered. "I have told you already that we possess powers beyond your imagination, including total control over your body, but still you make your futile attempts to break free from my grip."

This time the young man refused to allow the tears of fear to escape from his eyes. He had had quite enough of the humiliation and degradation he felt the night before, so he murmured quietly, "This is all a dream. I am certain."

"No, it is not a dream. I am your new reality, human – whether you like it or not."

The clear tone of confidence in that voice weakened his resolve. His heart quivered as he tried to imagine what sort of reality she meant.

"But why me, exactly?"

The voice did not reply, so a faint hope crept into his heart that he might be rid of the nightmare, especially since he had regained some movement in his fingertips. That hope was soon extinguished, however, when he noticed something far more dangerous. There, in the corner of the room opposite his bed, he saw an uncannily tall woman, with darkly tanned skin and curly, blazing hair, wrapped in a strange black rope!

He felt the blood freeze in his veins and the hair stand on his head. His eyes widened in horror and doubt about what he was seeing.

"What are you?" he asked.

She began to approach him, her pace torturously slow, until she got next to the bed. Then she leaned her upper body closer to him, so close he could see her face, which carried features similar to those of humans. But the pupils were red, and unlike human pupils, they were not round:

instead, they were thin and vertical – just like most species of snake.

The young man whimpered out loud as the awful visage drew ever closer, driving his fears to a new crescendo. This time the face moved its lips so he could hear the terrifying voice through his ears:

"Revenge. That is why, miserable one."

Then she was gone, leaving only a wave of frigid air that washed over his face. He still had not regained full control of his throat, so the piercing scream released itself, the sound of terror echoing off every wall in the house.

Chapter 11

By the time his parents rushed into the room, the paralysis had released its grip and he had stopped screaming. Now the screams were those of his horrified little brother.

The young man sat up in his bed, anxiously checking the room for the hateful woman and expecting to see her in one of the corners. Soon he felt certain that she was no longer there. He heaved a sigh of relief and told himself that it was just a nightmare, probably sparked by all the stress he had experienced on the ground floor.

His mother was now holding his younger brother, who calmed down in her arms, and his father came close to ask, "What happened, my son? Your scream scared us. Are you okay?"

He stared blankly at his father, trying not to let his face betray the inner conflict that he was going through: should he tell his parents all the details? Or was it better to keep the whole thing hidden and spare them any more distress?

"Why don't you answer?"

His mother's impatience forced him to take a decision, so he answered, "I'm sorry for waking you all up. It was just a stupid nightmare, really. I'm just embarrassed that I screamed like that."

As he had done after having heard him shouting on the ground floor, the father examined his son's features, trying to see if he was hiding something. Once again, he saw nothing conclusive, so he pressed for more information, giving his son an extra opportunity to reveal any secrets he was guarding.

"My dear boy, the last time you were talking to the void downstairs, and just now you were screaming hysterically. God knows what might happen the next time. Is there anything you'd like to tell us about so we can help you?"

The young man gave him a thin smile as he answered.

"Believe me, father, there's nothing worth being concerned about, just a strange nightmare. It's all the stress because final exams are approaching, and that's going to determine my future path."

His father gave him an encouraging pat on the shoulder and his mother offered some comforting words.

"You're a smart and hardworking student, may God protect you," she told him. "Someone like you shouldn't worry so much about passing the exams and determining the future. Try to relax and restore your focus."

"With God's will, mother. I apologize again for disturbing all of you and ruining your sleep. Have a good night."

He tried repeatedly to go back to sleep after his parents left the room, but to no avail. He went back to looking at the ceiling, silently reviewing the details of the nightmare. It was impossible not to ask himself the question. *Was it really a dream, or was it reality?* Then he pressed the spot under his chin again.

It still hurt.

Chapter 12

They were in Jeddah for their family visit when the father heard his pager go off, informing him that someone was trying to reach him. He frowned as he checked the number on the small screen, then asked his wife's mother if there was a telephone he could use in a quiet part of the flat. She led him out of the sitting room and down the hall to another room, then came back to rejoin her daughter, who rubbed her hands anxiously.

For the next few minutes, her eyes kept going back to the hallway. When her husband reappeared, he wore a pronounced frown on his face, and their son came in at the same time.

The wife sensed that something was wrong and was in a hurry to know more.

"I hope everything's is okay," she said. "Who sent you that call? Why do you look so bothered?"

Her husband heaved a long sigh and he threw his body into the nearest sofa, muttering, "There is no might or power but in God. All is according to God's will."

Her anxiety rising to a new level, she immediately got up and sat beside him, clutching his arm.

"What happened?" she asked. "Please tell me."

"The house," he said.

"The house? What about it?"

"It caught fire."

The wife and her mother gasped simultaneously, the older

woman covering her mouth with her hand. The young man's eyes narrowed, and he urged his father to give more details about what had happened.

"There isn't much to say for now. One of our neighbours says the smell of burning furniture was strong, and the smoke billowed heavily. He called the fire brigade, and they managed to put it out, thanks to God."

His son asked, "So was the whole house burnt? Are we homeless now?"

His father shook his head. "No, my son. It's not that bad. The fire burned most of the ground floor, but nothing else."

His mother-in-law tried to stress the positive.

"Thank God, thank God!" she exclaimed. "Its' such a great blessing that this happened whilst you were away from the house. Anything else can be replaced."

The young man turned back to his father, asking, "Dad, do you think the electrician did something wrong when he came yesterday?"

"That's the only logical explanation, son. I can't think of any other interpretation for what happened."

Then the father got up, saying, "Now I have to head back to Makkah to follow up on the incident. I'll see you tomorrow, God willing, if all goes well."

His wife hung onto his arm nervously. "Please take care of yourself," she said, "and call us whenever you have a chance."

He gave her a reassuring smile, stroked her arm, and left, not noticing the pained expression on his son's face. The young man soon left the sitting room, too, avoiding eye contact with both his mother and his grandmother as he made his way towards one of the small balconies. Once he got there, he pressed his wrist on the site of the pain, namely, below his chin.

PART II
THE ROOM AND THE HUMAN TIME BOMB

(Eastern Province 1993)

Chapter 13

The plane shuddered as its landing gear touched down on the tarmac, pulling Yusuf out of those disturbing memories of his last months in secondary school. He leaned over a bit to look at whatever he could see through the small window.

His best friend, Yaser, woke from a deep sleep just then, yawning hard before asking, "Have we finally arrived?"

Yusuf laughed. "You've spent the whole trip sleeping. God's will, no envy, but now you're asking about our arrival as if you spent the whole time waiting!"

Pale-skinned, plump-bodied, and nearly round-faced, Yaser wore a thin moustache, and his wavy, chestnut hair was always swept back. He laced his fingers together and stretched his arms out in front of himself, trying to loosen the stiffness in his muscles.

Only then did he answer, kiddingly, "My friend, it's not my fault that you're afraid of planes and can't sleep on one."

"I'm not afraid, Yaser. It's just a bit of anxiety and concern about the turbulence. Besides that, I find it hard to sleep sitting up."

Yaser teased him a little more: "Fine. Anxiety and concern. As you like."

The plane soon came to a complete stop, and the flight crew turned off the seatbelt sign, so they stood up, grabbed their carry-ons from the overhead compartment, and disembarked with the rest of the passengers. They headed into the small arrivals hall for domestic flights, and as they were waiting for their luggage, Yusuf zoned out again as he thought of the new life waiting for him here in Eastern Province, far from his parents. He would have to be in charge of his own affairs now, without their assistance and in a place where he knew no one except his brother Husam and his lifelong friend Yaser.

His raised his hand and lightly pressed his fingers on that spot under his chin. The pain was still there, but with far less severity than before, and the quick, raging headaches came less frequently. The strange thing was that after that night when the evil voice seemed to come to life inside his room, the nightmare had not come back. He was still thinking about that fact. *Does that constitute proof that the whole thing really was nothing but a silly dream?*

It was the mocking tone of Yaser's voice that brought him back to reality,

"Indeed, you only realize the value of the blessing when it's gone," his friend was saying. "I've always grumbled about the size of the airport in Jeddah, but compared to this, Jeddah's is big and beautiful!"

Yaser already had his luggage, and soon Yusuf retrieved his from the carousel as well. "May God be our guide," he said. "Let's go."

The two youths walked towards the exit, and when they got outside, they were met by a gust of the hot and humid sea air for which the area was known.

"Great, just what we were expecting," Yaser quipped. "Even the weather is against us here, my friend!"

That forced Yusuf to laugh as he waved for a taxi. Then he

asked, "Will you ever stop complaining?"

His friend laughed as he climbed into the backseat and answered, "I won't be Yaser anymore if I do."

Yusuf shook his head in mock desperation before sitting beside his friend and closing the door.

Chapter 14

"Thank God for your safe arrival," Husam cried as he embraced his brother, "and welcome to university life!"

Yusuf replied happily, "My dear brother, I've missed you so much! How are you doing here?"

Husam raised his hand to adjust the thick glasses above his nose and answered, "Fine, praise be to God. As I told you before, studying here is not easy at all, but for hardworking students who were high achievers at secondary school, there won't be any problems, God willing."

Husam was thin and light-skinned, his broad face was clean-shaven, and he combed his hair to the side. Yusuf was built along thicker lines, with tanned skin, a round face, and a moustache. Like Yaser, he brushed his hair straight back.

Husam extended his hand to his brother's friend, saying, "Hello, Yaser. How are you? You haven't changed much since the last time I saw you in Makkah."

Yaser shook his hand warmly and then looked around in wonder as he took in the details of the room.

"Do you really live here?!"

Husam laughed as he pulled out a couple of chairs for his guests and sat down on his bed.

"You're not the first student to be shocked at what student housing looks like," he said. "Nearly all of us had the same surprise, but you'll soon get used to everything here."

Yusuf asked, "Where is your room companion?"

ROOM NUMBER 8

"You mean my 'roommate,' Osama. He went to bring us all food from one of the most famous restaurants in the city. You are our guests today, so you must be well-hosted, as you know. He should be back soon, God willing," Hosam told them. "And now, please allow me to outline some basic things here. Yusuf, you'll know a lot of this because I've told you about it, but it won't hurt for you to hear it again. Repetition is beneficial."

Husam explained that all students who lived in the residence were to be regarded as roommates, and the building was divided into groups of rooms referred to as "halls." Each hall consisted of a standalone section, whether in a single line or U-shaped, with even-numbered rooms on one side of the corridor and odd numbers on the other. The basic living unit was a small room with basic furniture for two. Outside each hall, through an entrance with no door, was a section for toilets and shower stalls.

Here Yaser interrupted him by asking, somewhat incredulously, "The toilets and showers have no doors?"

Husam provided more details "The entrance to the section is basically just a hole in the wall, but each toilet room has a small door. As for the shower stalls, they are surrounded by walls on three sides and by plastic curtains on the fourth. I explained all this to Yusuf and my parents right after joining the university."

Yaser gave Yusuf a look of admonishment and cried, "Oh, man! You knew all this and didn't tell me?"

Yusuf shrugged his shoulders: "I'm sure you wouldn't have abandoned the idea of joining one of the top-ranked universities in the kingdom if I had told you. Do you know why I think that? Because I didn't, and you think exactly like me when it comes to your future."

Yaser admitted that everything his friend had said was true, so he immediately reined in his temper and moved to his next question.

"But if the toilets and showers aren't inside a modern building that insulates them from the weather outside, then how do you shower in winter when it's freezing outside?"

Husam answered, "Every student copes in his own way. There are some who take their personal stuff and head to the more modern student housing, which is allocated for the seniors, where they can enjoy a shower in a heated area. Others rent rooms in hotels or spend the weekend with their relatives from time to time for the same reason. And of course, there are some who have no choice but to stay here and wrestle the cold."

Before Husam could ask his next question or express distress at what he was learning about his new home, someone knocked on the door, so Husam called out, "Osama, is that you?"

"Yes."

The door was soon opened to a handsome young man with short black hair, a moustache, and an athletic build.

"Hello Yusuf and Yaser, praise be to God for your safety," he said as he walked in and laid out the plastic bags he was carrying onto the floor. "Husam has told me a lot about you."

Then he pulled a large plate made of light aluminium from its place between the two desks and placed it on the floor in the middle of the room, where he emptied the bags into it. A strong aroma filled the room, and Yaser commented, "Wow! The most famous foods here are nothing but Bukhari rice and grilled chicken?"

Osama released a pure, merry laugh as he kept preparing the place for meal-time, whilst Husam explained.

"Food was the second shock we all had after the residence itself, he said. "Enjoying fancy meals in luxurious restaurants is way beyond the budgets of most students."

Yusuf asked, "What about the university cafeteria?"

Osama shrugged his shoulders as he answered, "That choice is available, of course, but under two important conditions: you'll have to adjust to the strange flavour of the food it serves, and try to ignore the side-effects of the added ingredients."

"Added ingredients? What do you mean?"

"You'll get to know everything in time. Right now, stop asking questions, and let's start eating before the food gets cold."

The four sat around the big dish, and Yaser looked lost, so Husam asked if he was looking for something.

"Yes, a spoon," Yaser said. "Where are the spoons?"

Husam and Osama dug their hands into rice.

"Man, welcome again to student housing," Hosam said. "This is university life. You won't find anyone eating rice with a spoon here."

Chapter 15

Despite the description Husam had provided to the newcomers about an hour earlier, just looking at the toilets and showers section from the entrance gave them both a feeling of disgust

To the left, there were four small, worn-out doors, their eroded lower ends sending a clear message about the filth and neglect that waited inside. When they looked to the right, they saw what looked like four short corridors, lined up tightly, side by side, with a plastic curtain covering the entrance to each one. Each curtain was held in place by a thin metal rod. As for the washbasins, they stood in the middle of the section, a small square mirror above each one.

And because the section had no exterior door, it was filled with both flying and crawling insects, which joined humidity and pungent odours as permanent guests there. Yaser was astonished at what he saw.

"That's a million time worse than Husam's description," he said.

Yusuf walked in slowly and stood next to one of the basins as he looked around the place. He had to agree with his friend. "The conditions in here are miserable," he said. "I'm afraid that a snake or a scorpion might pop out any moment!"

Yaser followed him, standing before the adjacent basin. They both turned on the taps and proceeded to wash their hands and faces. Yaser started rinsing his mouth out with some water – and instantly spat it out.

"Ugh! What is that?" he exclaimed.

Yusuf froze in place and asked, "What happened?"

Yaser spat into the washbasin several more times before answering, his face a mask of distress.

"The water, man, the water!"

"What's wrong with it?!"

"It's really salty, like it came directly from the sea. It smells musty, too! Oh God, is this my punishment for making my father angry sometimes?"

Yusuf tried the water too, and with the same result. He spat it out. "How could anyone use that to rinse his mouth?"

The two silently pondered the water running from the taps for a few seconds. They were both in a state of denial until Yaser spoke up: "Yusuf, did we make a mistake by coming to this university?"

Before his friend could answer him, raucous laughter broke out behind them. They both spun around to see Osama and Husam, who said, with high amusement, "Guys, you are the consummate Oria!"

Yaser frowned. "Oria? What is that exactly?!"

Yusuf answered instead of his brother, "It's the term they use for first-year students. It comes from the English word "orientation," which means making someone ready for something new."

Yaser's voice seemed to overflow with resentment as he turned to his best friend and cried, "Are there any more shocks that you haven't told me about yet? Come on, Yusuf."

"Let me think. Hmm, the room, the toilets, the shower stalls, the food, the water ... I believe that's all."

Osama pointed at a spot outside the toilets and showers

section and corrected him: "No, Yusuf. You forgot something important here – the telephone!"

That got Yaser going even more.

"The telephone?" he asked. "What about it?"

"Haven't you told him about the telephone conditions here, Yusuf?"

Yusuf shook his head, and Husam took glee in explaining this part.

"There are only two fixed telephones here in these U-shaped halls, one for each side. That's not very many phones for all these rooms," he said. "But it gets better! Every student here has already arranged a certain time and day each week when his family can call, since there are no internal extensions. And since all the halls in the residence share a single outside telephone line, you have to wait forever if you want order food or call anywhere else!"

Yaser put his hand on his head and rolled his eyes. "Guys, this is looking like the worst decision of my entire life!"

Chapter 16

The next morning, Yusuf and Yaser followed Husam's directions to the small building that was home to Student Housing Affairs. They were supposed to be assigned a room, where they would spend the next couple of years before moving to the new residence buildings.

The lack of sleep was written all over their faces. The night before had been their first in this difficult new world, and they had spent it on the floor of Husam and Osama's room.

The building was not as crowded as they expected it to be, and they soon found themselves at the front of the queue, speaking through a small window with a clerk.

"Can I see your letters of acceptance please?" he asked.

They handed them what he had requested, along with national identity cards. Yusuf said, "We would be grateful if you could help us find a room in a hall near Number 620, where my brother resides."

The man checked through the pile of papers in front of him, and the longer it took, the more their anticipation turned to anxiety. Finally the clerk shook his head in resignation. "I'm sorry, but there are no vacancies in any of the blocks near that hall," he told them.

Yaser pursed his lips sorrowfully and commented, "What a pity. It's is a well-known fact that things don't always go as planned."

Yusuf agreed with a nod of his head, thinking how

unpleasant this development was, but then the man behind the window spoke again.

"Wait a minute. I think there's a single vacant room in Hall 621. That's next to your brother's residence. My apologies. I didn't see it at first. Our computer system recently went down, and it's difficult to manage and control such a large number of rooms manually, as you can see. I hope it'll come back online before the term starts next week."

The two students rejoiced at the news and the clerk handed them their keys, a diagram showing where their room was, and a sheet of paper.

"Just sign this to confirm receipt of the keys," he said. "I wish you all the best in your study journey."

Chapter 17

"There it is!"

Yaser pointed excitedly at the U-shaped block of rooms. Just as the man had said, it was located behind the block where Husam and Osama resided.

Yusuf wiped sweat off his face with tissue paper. "Luckily it wasn't hard to get here," he said, "and it's very close to my brother's place."

They continued walking until they reached the open corridor. They walked slowly, as if they were afraid to disturb the serenity of the place, but Yaser could not hold his grumbling for long, so he murmured, "What a gloomy hall. It looks like a prison!"

Yusuf shook his head at his friend's never-ending negativity, answering quietly, "That's not surprising. We experienced something similar yesterday in the other hall. Apparently this is just the way things are here."

The room numbers were on the doors, and all the even numbers were on his left. He was counting each one off as they passed it: "Number 2, Number 4, Number 6, ours should be next. Just let me double-check." He looked down at the diagram and re-examined his surroundings for a moment.

"Yes, this is it!" he declared at last, "Room Number 8!"

Yusuf reached into his pocket for the key, stuck it into the lock, and then completely froze. The memory of a very similar scene had suddenly pushed its way into his mind. He did not just remember being at the door to the ground floor at his father's house: he almost felt like he was there. Even the chill and the racing of his heart were identical to what he had experienced back in Makkah. He quickly drifted off into his innermost thoughts. *What does this mean?*

"Eight has been my favourite number since childhood," Yaser noted happily, for once taking a positive view of things, "and now it follows me to my room number at uni ... What? Is there a problem with the lock? Yusuf, what's wrong with you?"

The question brought Yusuf back to reality, so he quickly turned the key, and they both heard the sound of the lock behaving as it should.

"Don't worry, Yaser. The lock is fine and so am I. I just zoned out for a second, that's all."

"Then try not to zone out too often, my friend. We need our full concentration at this stage of our lives."

Yusuf sighed out loud but nodded his head in agreement. Part of him wished he could share the secret he was hiding with his best friend, but he had decided that day in Makkah to not tell anyone about it.

He pushed the door open slowly, so the hinges squeaked, intensifying the chill he felt inside. Despite his apprehension, he entered the room with Yaser close behind.

It was perfectly identical to the room Husam and Osama shared. A large wardrobe was fixed to the wall directly on the left, extending from floor to ceiling. After the wardrobe came three wooden shelves that were also fixed to the wall above a brown wooden desk with a chair nestled between its legs. On the wall opposite the door, there was a small rectangular window, complete with a suitably sized cloth curtain, that overlooked the street. Beneath it lay a bed and beside it an air conditioner. The third wall was where the second desk and chair were placed, and on the last wall, to the right, another small window looked into the corridor, with the second bed below it.

Both young men were engulfed by strong feelings as they stood silently in the middle of the room. Yaser refrained comment on the drear of the place, which almost drew tears as he contemplated the idea of spending two years in such a depressing little space. Yusuf was preoccupied with something else, wrestling with his chills and unease and wondering why they had returned at this particular moment. He soon snapped out of it, however, blaming himself for the brief bout of anxiety and heading towards the opposite wall, where he turned on the air conditioner.

It came to life with a loud buzz that banished the silence from the room.

"Great!" Yaser said. "I can't wait to experience studying and sleeping with that special sort of authentic music!"

Yusuf went to the nearest desk and swept his forefinger over its surface, leaving a clear mark in the layer of dust that covered it. Deep inside, he couldn't blame his friend for grumbling, since the latter was right: it did not look like the coming days would be easy at all. Nonetheless, they had to keep their focus on what it would take to adapt and get used to it rather than giving in to the shock and disappointment.

"May God be our guide, Yaser," he said. "Now, let's follow my brother's advice and organize our schedule so we can carry out the necessary tasks."

Yaser raised his fingers one by one, ticking off what needed to be done: "Bring a worker to clean the room, transfer our luggage from Husam and Osama's room, organize our clothes and stuff, pick up the cars, then go shopping for household items and a small refrigerator. Is that everything?"

Yusuf was already pulling the door open as he looked over his shoulder and nodded his head in agreement, and when he turned towards the corridor he gasped, recoiling instinctively as he realized that someone was standing just outside the doorway.

Chapter 18

"Sorry, boss! I didn't mean to startle you. It's just that the room has been empty for so long, and I wanted to see the new faces who are moving in."

The young man in the corridor wore embarrassment on his face. He was a tall, dark-skinned guy with short, curly hair and a round face, and his beard and moustache were neatly trimmed. He had no shirt on, revealing a solid build.

"No problem," Yusuf told him. "I was just busy talking to my friend and wasn't paying attention. I'm Yusuf, and this is Yaser. We're first-year preparatory students."

The guy greeted him warmly, saying, "Welcome to your new home. I'm Ashraf, your neighbour in Number 6. I've finished my first two years. It seems from your accent that you're from the western part of the kingdom. So am I – from Makkah to be precise."

Yaser came forward when he heard that, leaving the room to greet their new neighbour.

"That's great," he said "We're from Makkah too. I'm sure having a neighbour from our hometown will ease the homesickness, but tell me, do all students here walk around bare-chested, wearing only shorts?"

Ashraf chuckled at the new guy. "I just woke up and was on my way to use the toilet and take a shower," said. "Anyway, you'll soon find out that each student has his own norms and his own approach to life."

Yaser pointed at his own chest and said, "Perfect, that would be my approach too, wearing nothing but shorts!"

Yusuf looked at his friend with genuine surprise, whilst Ashraf laughed again and patted Yaser on the shoulder saying, "I like your sense of humour, my neighbour. You'll need it to cope with the difficulties here. And now, allow me to be on my way. As you know, the call of nature cannot be ignored for long."

Yusuf replied, "Actually, this is a good opportunity to explore the condition of the toilets and showers. We saw a very discouraging sample yesterday in Hall 620, where my brother lives."

The three walked along the empty corridor and Yaser asked, "What about your roommate?"

"His name is Bassam, really nice guy from here in Eastern Province. I met him by chance at the housing office and we got along right away, so we agreed to share a room. It was such a relief to feel so comfortable after just a few minutes of talking, if you know what I mean. He spends the weekends at his family home, then comes back with lots of food and delicious desserts, all prepared by his mother, may God protect her."

Yaser was impressed: "So you eat clean, home-made food every week. Man, you're lucky!"

They reached the entrance to the toilets and showers, which had the exact same design as Husam and Osama's. Ashraf continued inside whilst Yusuf and Yaser scanned the place in disappointment. The latter muttered, "Screwed. I was hoping it might be better here, but it's even worse!"

Chapter 19

The day passed quickly for Yusuf and Yaser, which was no surprise, given all the things they had to get done. First, they found and hired an Asian worker to clean the room, then they retrieved their luggage and organized their clothes and other possessions. Next, Osama took them to the shipping company where their cars were waiting for them. They then went shopping for a refrigerator, some groceries, and a long list of other supplies.

Now, they were back in the room and it was almost nine in the evening. Yaser took a small square mirror with a plastic handle and frame from one of the boxes and held it at the same height as his face as he looked around the room. He then took a few steps towards the three shelves against the wall, trying to choose between the lower and middle shelves.

"What are you doing?" Yusuf asked.

Yaser answered without lowering his arms or taking his eyes off the mirror: "This is the best place for it. We don't need to fix it with screws, and the height is very convenient to see the face. If only the mirror were just a few millimetres shorter, it would be a perfect fit between the shelves."

Despite realizing that the mirror was bigger than the gap between the shelves, Yaser did not give up. He kept pressing the edges of the mirror, trying to wedge it into place. He eventually succeeded, but just as he did, the frame cracked.

Still Yaser was undeterred. "Finally," he said, "but I think it's stuck."

He tried repeatedly to pull it out, but to no avail.

Yusuf had lost patience. "See what your brilliant idea did? How we are supposed to get it out now?"

"Who said we wanted to take it out now?" his friend asked. "If God blesses us with long lives and the time comes for us to leave this room, then we can look into that international case! Deal?"

Yusuf sighed in exasperation, then sat on the floor and started spreading out a small plastic sheet to eat off of. "Whatever, let's eat."

They sat on the floor and ate sandwiches with their eyes fixed on the screen of their new television, which they had temporarily placed on one of the desks. They were watching the local broadcast of a football match after several failed attempts to get the satellite reception working.

Suddenly, Yusuf felt pain under his chin, and the next moment they heard something crashing to the floor behind them. They both flinched at the noise and turned to see what had happened.

Yaser was perplexed at what they saw. "The teapot! How could it just fall off the top of the fridge like that?"

Yusuf tried not to be spooked. He kept chewing and offered a couple of possibilities. "It must have been right on the edge, or maybe it wasn't level and the air pushed around by the AC was enough to blow it over."

Yaser frowned thoughtfully for a few seconds, then shook his head. "Neither this nor that," he insisted. "I'm sure I left it standing straight, and nowhere near the edge – almost in the middle!

ROOM NUMBER 8

Then he shrugged his shoulders, threw up his hands in surrender, and went back to his sandwich and the game.

But not Yusuf. He had stopped chewing when he heard how certain his friend was about where the pot had been. He shuddered as a quick chill swept over him, and when he finally started to eat again, he did so slowly and absentmindedly.

Chapter 20

"Good night."

It was almost midnight, and Yaser had not so much spoken the words as yawned them. He was exhausted and would soon be fast asleep. Yusuf replied in kind but kept staring at the ceiling, lost in thought about so much that had happened.

Everything had started back there on the ground floor of his father's house, where disturbance had come over him for no apparent reason, followed by that violent blow to his face, then the peculiar dreams, and soon after that, a fire had consumed that part of the house whilst he and his family were away.

And now here, on their first day inside the room, the teapot falls off the fridge, all by itself, without any logical explanation. He was troubled by the questions that came to mind. *How could it have fallen? And is there a connection between what happened in Makkah and what's happening now?*

He brought his fingers up beneath his chin, as if they could answer his questions. He pressed gently and felt a slight pain.

Chapter 21

Despite all the insights and preparation that Husam and Ashraf had provided about the first official day of the preparatory year, going through it in person was a memorably difficult experience for both Yusuf and Yaser.

They started with the long queues in front of the preparatory year building to get their schedules, then waited again to get the required books. There followed an overwhelming rush, back and forth between different floors trying to obtain approvals to get into the right sections and study groups, all the while lugging all of their books around. Like many students, it was on their first real day of university that they learned the true meaning of the word "hectic."

By the time they got back to the room, it was almost sundown. They unloaded the heavy books onto their desks and laid down on their respective beds to rest their weary bodies. Yaser moaned aloud. Yusuf stretched his arms and legs out and on the bed and heard his friend start to grumble, "Once again, today I came to the realization that my decision to come here was totally wrong! Why do they have to make us suffer all day?"

Yaser got no reply from Yusuf, but Ashraf had just let himself in and watched them collapse onto their beds.

"You're such weak *Oria* guys!" he teased. "God help you."

Neither of the neophytes could summon the energy to get up to greet him, but Yusuf smiled apologetically. "Hello

Ashraf. Come in, and please excuse us for not getting up."

"I'm the one who owes you an apology for breaking into your room," he said with a smile, "but the door was left ajar, and I couldn't resist coming in to chat with you about your first day!"

Ashraf had just settled into the nearest chair when they all heard a light knock on the door. Yusuf called out, "Come in, please."

Husam pushed the door open and entered the room, where he was introduced to Ashraf and then immediately started inspecting the place.

"So, this is Room Number 8, which had been locked up for long? Hmm ... It's an exact copy of our room, but it's rather cold! It seems that the air conditioner is doing its job. How was your first day?"

Yusuf and Yaser explained what they had faced, and Husam nodded his head considerately. "The first-day misery is still as it was," he commented. "Praise be to God for the good and the bad."

The conversation had pulled both Yusuf and Yaser into sitting positions by the time a knock on the door signalled the arrival of a third guest. This time it was Bassam, who was introduced to everyone by Ashraf, and they all stood to greet him. Then Yaser piped up.

"Oh, Ashraf, you found a roommate who's as tall as you are? That must have taken some effort!"

Everyone chuckled. Bassam was indeed very tall, and very skinny, too. His skin was very dark, and he sported a thick moustache, as well as a shaped and lighter beard. "Nice to meet you all, guys," he said in deep but quiet voice. "Ashraf told me that two new guys have arrived in Room Number 8, so I decided to welcome them my way. Excuse me for a moment."

With that he left the room. He was back very soon, however, this time with a large dish with several pieces of cake – some vanilla, some chocolate – neatly aligned on top.

He happily explained: "I asked my mother, may God protect her, to make twice as much cake this time, so come on, help yourselves, boys. Bon appétit!"

Everyone accepted the invitation. Yaser was especially appreciative – and already thinking ahead to future feeds.

"Yusuf and I are so lucky!" he said through a mouthful of cake. "We won't be completely deprived of the joy of eating home-made food!"

Yusuf glared at him for his presumptuousness, but Bassam smiled broadly.

"It's no problem," he said, noting Yusuf's embarrassment. "I bring stuff from home at the beginning of every week, and I'll make sure to bring some extra for you guys."

But Yusuf did not want to be seen as taking advantage of the new neighbour he had just met.

"Bassam," he said, "please don't bother yourself or your mother like that."

Bassam's lips opened to reply, but Ashraf was faster: "Don't worry man. Our kind Prophet had recommended being kind to neighbours both near and far, and you're living in the room right next to ours! Plus, my experience with Bassam's family leaves no doubt how kind and generous they are."

Chapter 22

Once everyone had left and quiet returned to the room, it was not long before Yaser sank into the seas of sleep, whilst Yusuf lay on his side next to the small window that overlooked the corridor.

His body was just starting to relax when he heard the sound of a few light knocks on the window, instantly alerting all of his senses. Holding his breath, he raised his head and listened intently to make sure he had not imagined it. He heard the sound again, so there was no way he was mistaken, but he wondered who would be knocking on his window at that time of night.

Yusuf slowly pulled the curtain aside. The window was made of smoked glass that prevented a clear view, but he could still make out a shadow on the other side. Immediately, he felt the familiar pain under his chin.

He had to know who – or what – was out there, so he quickly sat up and turned the knob to open the window. His vision unobstructed, he looked into the corridor again. No one.

He frowned in frustration, but he also acted without delay. He turned to Yaser to ask if he had heard anything, but his friend was clearly sleeping like a baby, so he quickly shut the window and rushed to the door. He pulled it open and was soon standing in the corridor, looking around to see who had tapped on the window.

The corridor was completely empty and quiet, and their

room was in the middle of its length, so there had been no time for a practical joker or anyone else to have got out of sight that fast. Yaser wondered if he were dreaming.

He sighed wearily and went back to bed after making sure that both the door and the window were securely locked.

Chapter 23

A few days after they had moved in, Yusuf and Yaser received a visitor. He introduced himself as Mansour, explaining that he was a third-year student and the person in charge of student affairs for their hall. He officially welcomed them to the residence and said he needed to verify some information sent to him from the housing office. The two greeted him formally and Yusuf invited him to sit. He was heavyset, with light skin, a long beard, and a sharpened moustache.

"So you're Yusuf and Yaser," Mansour said as he sat down. "Can I see your national identity cards, please?"

They handed him the cards and he went through the verification process quickly, then starting explaining a number of rules for those living inside the block. They learned very little that Husam and Osama had not already told them, even exchanging a meaningful look to this effect, but there was no point saying this to the head of their block and possibly getting off on the wrong foot by making him feel embarrassed. Yusuf gave Yaser a short, sharp glance, silently warning him to hold his tongue.

Mansour noticed none of this as he was busy organizing the papers he was reading from. When he was finished, he said, "Do you know what, Yaser? You have such a special student number!"

Yaser lifted his eyebrows out of curiosity.

"A special number? How is that?"

ROOM NUMBER 8

Mansour pointed at a specific point on one of the papers, saying: "Look. Your number is nine-three-six-two-one-eight, but if we break it down a certain way, we get ninety-three, which is the year you joined the university, then six hundred and twenty-one, which is the number of this hall, and finally, the number eight, which is your room number! Isn't that amazing? You must be the only student in the history of the university whose student number is also his address here!"

Yaser looked duly surprised and impressed.

"Wow! I hadn't noticed at all, and that IS a strange coincidence," he said. "You made my day, boss. That's at least some compensation for some of the difficulties and disastrous conditions we've seen here."

Mansour laughed as he stood up. He patted Yaser on the shoulder and excused himself, but before he could leave, Yusuf had a question:

"Could you please tell us why this room was kept closed for a longer period of time than usual?"

Mansour was obviously upset by the question. He frowned and started to leave without answering, but as he opened the door, he stopped and looked over his shoulder at both them.

"Any room in any hall can stay empty for an indefinite period of time because the choice of rooms is conducted randomly in most cases, unless a preference is indicated for a certain spot," he said. "Now you'll have to excuse me as I have lots to do. If you need anything, please don't hesitate to come see me. I'm in Number 5. Goodbye."

Mansour left the room and closed the door behind him. Yusuf and Yaser heard his steps getting further away until the silence resumed.

Chapter 24

"Are you still awake, Yaser?" Yusuf asked that night as he lay on his bed, staring at the ceiling again.

"Sure, I'm awake."

"What are you thinking about?"

"The same thing you're thinking about."

Yusuf heaved a deep sigh, then said: "A room that was empty for a long time, where a teapot falls all by itself on our first day in it, and it so happens that its address matches your student number, and then the head of the hall dodges a question about it. What does all of this mean?"

"It may mean a lot, and it may mean nothing."

"And to which of these two possibilities would you tend to subscribe?"

"The first, but my mind pushes me towards the second because we shouldn't make hasty judgments about what's going on. They could all be mere coincidences."

"If that was your thought, then what's keeping you awake like this?"

It was Yaser's turn to heave a deep sigh. Then he answered:

"Curiosity is killing me, my friend. I want to know the story behind this room. What about the two students before us? Where did they go? And why did it stay empty for such a long time?"

Chapter 25

"It's such a long and harrowing story."

That was how Ashraf initially answered as he sipped from the cup of tea in his hands. He was sitting on his bed with his back against the wall to face Yusuf and Yaser, the former seated on a chair and the latter on the other bed as Bassam was away.

After more than a week, they finally had the time for a proper conversation with Ashraf to ask him about the story behind their room. Now they were excited after he indicated that he knew that story.

"We're all ears," said Yaser. "Please tell us."

Ashraf paused for a bit as he pondered the cup in his hands, as though he were retrieving the memories. Then he took another sip and began to tell the tale.

"The last two students who lived in your room were Wahid and Mashaal," he said. "They were weirdos and had weird ideas. It was obvious from their outer appearance and the way they dealt with all the people around here, so everyone avoided them. Especially since they made no effort to hide the sins they used to commit inside the room."

Ashraf paused when he saw looks of both condemnation and incredulity in his friends' eyes. He nodded his head in confirmation and continued.

"I know it's hard to believe, but this is what happened. The sounds and music of pornographic films, the filthy jokes and insults they exchanged ... Whoever was in the corridor could hear everything."

Yaser interrupted, "Oh, man! What are you saying? Were these things reported to the administration?"

"We reported what was going on to Mansour, who was already the head of the hall, so he visited the two guys in their room as an initial procedure, hoping they'd stop. But then he asked everyone who lived here to ignore them and not raise any complaints against them to the university."

Now it was Yusuf's turn to interrupt: "He said to ignore them? Why? That makes absolutely no sense!"

"Indeed, and no one was able to figure out what caused the transformation in Mansour's attitude! And this was nothing. Things with the guys got even worse after that."

Yaser was appalled. "Things got worse? What's worse than what you've just described?"

Ashraf nodded solemnly, a look of distress etched on his face.

"A lot worse than anyone in student housing has ever done before," he said. "They ended up smuggling a prostitute onto campus in their car and sneaking her into Room Number Eight! I don't need to explain what the three of them got up to, do I?"

Now Yusuf and Yaser were even more shocked and disgusted by what had taken place – and right there in the room they now occupied. Their reactions were simultaneous, two streams of words that mixed together, making it difficult for Ashraf to hear who had said what:

"Huh?"

"What did you say?"

"No way!"

"Man ... there must be some kind of mistake."

Ashraf shook his head and gestured to the wall that separated their rooms. "My wall is the same wall as your room, and there was no sound insulation installed when they built this hall, so I could hear voices and everything else very clearly," he said. "Also, in the early morning after the incident with the prostitute, I came out my room as they were sneaking her out. She was dressed in a man's *thobe* and veiled with a *keffiyeh*. It was a huge shock to me, and for everyone else here."

Yusuf kept shaking his head.

"No might nor power but from God," he said. "And what about Mansour? Did his attitude finally change after that?"

"He visited them again in the room after he had heard the news," Ashraf replied, "but he left even more determined that we should neither confront them, nor report them to the administration!"

Chapter 26

After their chat with Ashraf had ended, Yusuf and Yaser went back to their room, and neither said a word for quite some time. They had a whole new – and deeply unsettling – perspective on their surroundings now and were too busy scanning the walls, the corners, and the furniture with their eyes. All they could think about was that everything Ashraf had told had taken place right here in their room.

When Yusuf had asked what happened to Wahid and Mashaal and how they ended up leaving the room, the tale had become even more disturbing. Ashraf said the two had eventually begun to isolate themselves in the room to carry out bizarre rituals. Each time, the rituals were accompanied by screams and cries from inside the room at different times of the night.

Finally, Mashaal rushed out of the room one night in a mad frenzy, got into his car and drove off. He had been in no state to drive, and soon the news came that he had been in an accident, sustaining injuries that would prove fatal. As for Wahid, Ashraf said he suffered a total breakdown and when the police came, they found a significant amount of drugs, so he was moved to a special facility where they treat mental illness and addiction. That was when the room was closed, and it had remained unoccupied ever since.

So that was what had happened, and Yusuf and Yaser no

longer felt lucky to have found a spot close to Husam and Osama. As the first students to reside there after Wahid and Mashaal, all either of them could think about now was what might be waiting for them in Room Number 8.

It was Yaser who spoke first. "Great! Now I'm living in a room that has witnessed all sorts of sins and deviant rituals, plus one of the two guys who used to live here died in a car accident, and the other one ended up in an addiction treatment centre. Sounds exciting!"

Yaser's outburst not only aggravated the pain under Yusuf's chin, but also doused him in so much negativity that he felt a strong urge to cry. Nonetheless, he summoned all his strength and tried to encourage his friend with a pat on the shoulder.

"I totally agree with you about the whole sordid story of Wahid and Mashaal," Yusuf said. "It's not an easy thing to digest. "But we need to do our best to keep our spirits high and keep moving forward. We'll never be able to graduate if we get distracted by this kind of thing."

Yaser gave him a look of deep gratitude and even managed a faint smile as he replied, "May God be our guide. Thank you very much, Yusuf, for the emotional support."

Then he felt a sudden chill. He rubbed his arms with his hands to warm up and motioned to the air conditioner, saying, "It seems like the only good thing about the room is that old AC. It's actually fascinating how effective it is!"

Chapter 27

A few days later, Yusuf headed down the corridor for a shower, his towel draped around his neck and a bag of toiletries swinging from his hand.

It was evening, and an autumn breeze gave him a slight chill as soon as he entered the showers area. He hesitated, inspecting his surroundings apprehensively, then took a deep breath and proceeded to one of the shower stalls, ignoring the mild pain under his chin. He slung his towel on the overhead rod and, not bothering to open the shower curtain, tossed the bag inside the stall. Then he turned to the basin opposite and started washing his hands. Lifting his gaze to the mirror, he was startled to find more than his own reflection: he also saw the blurred face of a woman who seemed to be watching him through the semi-transparent shower curtain!

He gasped and shuddered at the surprise, not moving a muscle except to blink his eyes to make sure his vision was clear. *But that's impossible,* he thought to himself. *How could there be a woman in here?*

He turned around as quickly as he could, hoping to confirm directly what he saw in the mirror. But there was no one there.

Annoyed and confused, he turned back to the mirror but now found nothing there, either. He frowned. *What was that? Have I started hallucinating all a sudden?* He heard a

noise that seemed to come from behind the shower curtain.
No, I'm not hallucinating.

He turned to face the shower curtain again, eyeing it suspiciously as his heart raced. He stepped slowly towards the stall, mind racing too: *I'm not imagining it, there really is something behind the curtain, but what could it be? And am I ready to face it?*

He gathered his courage. And then with a single motion, moving as fast he could, he took a final step forward, grabbed the curtain, and flung it to the side to uncover the whole stall. Despite having steeled himself, what he saw was such a shock that he let out a quick scream.

There in the middle of the stall stood a tall, thin woman whose ragged clothes showed her arms and legs, but whose long, straight hair fell loosely over her face, obscuring half of it. "Who are you?" Yusuf asked in an unsteady voice. "And how did you get in here?"

She stared at him coldly with her one uncovered eye. Instead of answering his question, she raised her arm and lifted her hair away, revealing that the other side of her face was an unspeakable horror. Her skin was torn in several places, parts of her skull were exposed, and she was missing an eye, the hollow socket holding only bloody scraps of flesh.

Before Yusuf could fully register what he was seeing, the woman lunged at him with surprising speed. He screamed again, closing his eyes instinctively as he shielded his face with his arms and retreated into a crouch, hoping to protect himself when she reached him.

But nothing happened.

He cautiously opened his eyes and, seeing no one, slowly stood up from the crouch and lowered his arms. He remained on guard in case the woman somehow attacked from another direction, but she was nowhere to be seen. He looked around and saw nothing until he cast his eyes downward: there on the floor of the stall in front of him stood a black cat. It was looking straight at him, and for moment he was sure it contorted its tiny mouth into a mocking smile. *Get a hold on yourself,* he thought. *That's impossible!*

Before he could decide what he was seeing, let alone what to do next, the cat bolted past him and through the entrance to the showers area, and then ran outside, where it was soon out of sight. Just as it did so, another student walked into the showers the same way the cat had left. Yusuf greeted him perfunctorily, than asked, "That cat that just left, does it live here?"

The student seemed surprised by the question. "What cat?"

"The black one that left just as you came in. It must have crossed right in front of you."

The student shook his head insistently. "Believe me, I didn't see a thing," he said. "Now if you'll excuse me ... "

The student went into one of the toilet rooms, leaving a thoroughly shocked Yusuf to his confusion. All he could think was that he must have been hallucinating.

Chapter 28

"Man, are you sure of what you're saying?" Yaser asked after his friend told him about the apparently disappearing cat but purposely left out the part about the hideously injured woman.

It was nearly midnight, and the sounds of nocturnal insects easily penetrated inside the residential block. Both Yaser and Yusuf were sitting on their beds, facing each other.

"I'm certain of what I saw," Yusuf replied. "A black cat walked right in front me, right before my eyes, and then left as the guy was coming in. How could he not have seen it?"

Yaser clapped his palms together in puzzlement, saying, "I don't know, but the whole thing is weird, especially considering what I witnessed yesterday."

Yusuf raised his eyebrows at that. "What? What happened? And why haven't you told me until now?"

Yaser hesitated a little, as though making up his mind. Then he spoke.

"I didn't think there was anything worth telling," he explained." Anyway, when I left the toilet, I could hear a cat meowing continuously, so I followed the sound to one of the washbasins. There was a pot underneath, and inside I saw a grey cat. She was wriggling in a strange way, and I've always loved cats, so I put my hand on her to see if I could provide a little comfort, but she ran quickly outside. There were three other students right around me when it happened, but none of them seemed to notice!"

He stopped there, so Yusuf commented anxiously, "Yes, that's what I mean. It's like no one can see cats except us. How can that be?"

"I have no answer."

"I have a possible explanation, but it sounds crazy."

"So what? I want to know, even if it's just out of curiosity."

Yusuf looked around the room before he answered. "Maybe the room has something to do with this, because of all the sick stuff that happened in here. It's the only thing that distinguishes us from the rest of the students here: we're both living here this room now"

Yaser yawned as he repositioned himself to lay down on his back.

"I had no idea you had such a vivid imagination," he said. "How could there be a relationship between a room and some people not being able to see cats? You said yourself it was a crazy idea. Come on, please. We have lectures early tomorrow, so let's get to sleep. Good night."

Soon he was snoring, whilst Yusuf kept staring at the ceiling for some time, the same unanswered question resonating in his head over and over again.

Why does no one see cats except us?

Chapter 29

Several weeks passed without anything strange happening again. Neither of the two cats, the black and the grey, had shown its face again.

Then one night, Yusuf woke from a sound sleep for no apparent reason. It was well after midnight, but he had no idea what time it was, or why he had woken up so suddenly. He felt dizzy and disoriented but also strangely alert, finally asking himself, in the faintest of voices, "What happened to me?"

And then an answer: "Obviously my presence surprises you."

His heart quivered at the sound of the feminine but somehow serpentine voice. Instantly he felt desperately afraid, besieged by a storm of terror that made his whole body tingle and then go numb, including that spot under his chin.

She was back. The same demon that had tortured him in Makkah, and just like the last time, Yusuf was paralyzed. This time he was on his left side, his back almost flush against the wall next to his bed.

Then he became aware of an odd sensation, one he had never experienced before. Something was hovering above and behind him, just beyond his field of vision. A being, one he could not see but whose presence could be felt, just as clearly as though a flesh-and-blood person were sitting next to him on the bed. He tried to scream from his lungs, but there was only a grieving silence. Both fear and curiosity demanded that he turn his head to have a look, but …

"Do not waste your time. You will not be able to move."

Whatever is it was behind him, he could feel it getting closer and closer until an unfamiliar pain coursed through his body, starting from the back of his neck and quickly reaching his heels.

"Is your memory that weak?" The sound of the female in his head voice was even angrier and more intense than before. "Let me refresh it for you."

Yusuf was instantly stricken by an agonizing headache. The demon really did have total control over his body, he realized, and she had a vicious temper!

"Oh, Yes!" he said. "I remember the word 'revenge.' But why? What did I do to deserve your revenge?"

The headache vanished at once, and Yusuf focused on catching his breath as the bloodcurdling voice spoke again:

"I am retaliating for my brother, human, my brother whose body was fatally damaged because of you."

"Because of me? How? When?"

"Do not play innocent. You know exactly what you did to my brother. I can ruin your internal organs and kill you at any moment I choose, but I will rather enjoy torturing you first. And I will make sure that this continues for an extended period, just like you made my brother suffer for so long from his burnt skin."

Before Yusuf could respond, he heard Yaser cough. He could not see because of the paralysis that kept him from moving his head, but he could still hear as his friend got out of bed, walked to the small refrigerator, open it, and take out a bottle of water. Then he unscrewed the cap and drank voraciously before heading back to his bed.

"We will meet again, you wretch. I promise you!"

The angry female voice faded away with that final threat, taking the numbness and spasm with it. Her departure was accompanied by the sound of breaking glass as something fell to the floor somewhere inside the room.

Having regained control over his body as soon she left, Yusuf sat up on his bed and stretched out his arm to turn the lights on. They both shut their eyes as light flooded the room, and it took several seconds to adjust.

When they could see again and realized what is was that had shattered on the floor, Yaser's eyes widened in astonishment, whilst Yusuf's whole body trembled uncontrollably.

Chapter 30

Once the initial shock had passed, Yaser cleaned up the shards of glass with the small vacuum cleaner they had bought shortly after moving in. Meanwhile, Yusuf bagged what remained of the mirror and its square frame, taking care not to drop any more pieces of glass onto the floor. He headed outside and dropped the bag into the large dumpster on the street near the housing block.

He then trudged back to the room with the weary steps of a worried mind.

Yaser was sitting on his bed his back against the wall, his expression reflecting the same agitation. He asked his friend, "What logical reason could there be to explain how that mirror fell the way it did," he asked, "keeping in mind that it was jammed between the shelves so tightly that I couldn't pull it out, no matter how hard I tried?"

Yusuf quickly searched for a scientific explanation. "Maybe the plastic frame shrank because the AC made the room so cold, so it was no longer held in place by the shelves, and when it fell over, the handle was pointed outward, which pulled it over the edge," he said.

That might be the reason," Yusuf added, but his tone suggested that even he found the theory unconvincing.

Yaser considered his fiend's idea and allowed that it was possible to some extent, but he also recalled an earlier event. "What about the teapot, " he asked, "which decided to commit suicide by throwing itself off the fridge whilst we were eating? Did it shrink too?"

Despite his distress, Yusuf laughed a little inside at Yaser's comment. The fact of the matter was that they couldn't account for what happened. He looked around the room for a while, then met his best friend's gaze. When he finally answered, he spoke slowly and deliberately.

"I have no other explanation except to say that this room is haunted," he said. "But is it reasonable to jump to such a conclusion so quickly?"

Yaser covered his face with his hands for a few seconds. Then he ran his fingers through his hair and turned his head left and right, as though searching for some detail they may have overlooked, something that would resolve the mysterious occurrences they had experienced. Finding none, he voiced mounting distress.

"So it's not enough being away from our families and living in this disgusting hall whilst trying to study for some really difficult courses? Now we have to worry about this room and the weird stuff going on here?" he said, clearly overwhelmed. "This was all we needed here! Oh God, have mercy on us."

The knocking started as soon as Yaser finished. It was light, but both young men could hear it, and Yusuf panicked.

"No! Not again!" he shouted.

The knocking was coming from the window near his bed – and it did not stop.

Now Yaser was doubly spooked, asking, "What do you mean, 'again'? What are these knocks?"

Yusuf did not answer right away. Instead, he held his breath, hoping that the sound would stop.

But it continued. Persistent. Urgent.

Yusuf finally answered, his voice cracking as pointed at the window: "I don't know. I heard it before, but when I went to the corridor, there was no one there!"

Yaser literally sprinted to the door, flung it open, and rushed into the corridor, his head turned to the left, where the window was, and his voice roaring:

"Who's the ... "

He swallowed hard, the rest of his words stopping in his throat as he realized that the corridor was empty.

Yaser shuffled back into the room. He shut the door behind him, but more out of habit than anything else: he could not believe what had just happened, and his mind was very much elsewhere. He heard Yusuf's voice – "You didn't find anyone, did you?" – but could not respond.

Yaser's movements were slow, but his heart beat rapidly as he approached his bed without looking at his friend. Even when he spoke, he did not answer the question. Instead, he started with one of his own:

"Were those really knocks on the window? Maybe we misinterpreted the whole thing. Maybe it was just some random noise from a distant source, something that has nothing to do with us. There are many buildings around us, and this hall directly overlooks the street."

This time it was Yaser's turn to be unconvinced by his own attempt to explain the inexplicable. Without waiting for an answer, he climbed back into his bed and pulled the blanket over himself, showing his back to his friend. Yusuf sighed sadly and lay down hesitantly on his own bed. He pressed the spot under his chin, and the pain gave him an answer all its own.

Chapter 31

Between what they had heard about the history of their room and the strange things they had witnessed there first-hand, the combination threw the two roommates into something of a funk over the next few weeks. They were both apprehensive and distracted, often zoning out in class. The idea of the room being haunted and the risks that might entail had taken over their minds.

Had Yaser been able to read his friend's mind, he would have known that Yusuf carried an additional burden, the one that revolved around his attempts to understand the mystery of the female demon who claimed he had harmed her brother. His fear was only exacerbated by the anger he felt at his inability to figure out the truth. The not knowing was eating away at his gut because he had no clue when she would attack next, or what might make her leave him alone. *There's nothing I can do but wait ...*

"You there, in the back ... Yusuf! I'm sure you can present the correct answer to the question. Please share it with us."

The maths professor's sarcasm reached into Yusuf's agonizing reverie and pulled him back into the harsh reality of the lecture hall. Once the initial confusion passed, he actually knew the answer, but the embarrassment stuck, making him nervous and self-conscious. He could only stutter when he tried to speak, so the professor interrupted:

"Stay with us during the lecture, Yusuf. Focus and concentrate."

Yusuf could only nod in assent as he broke into a cold sweat, mortified at the looks directed him by teacher and students alike.

With everyone's focus going back on the maths lesson, a fire of resentment flared inside Yusuf, and he silently damned the demon for the latest misery she had caused him.

Chapter 32

The following few weeks of the first term passed quickly. The timeline was tight, as students' schedules were packed with exams, and everyone devoted their energies to studying in hopes of achieving the best possible results.

As for Yusuf and Yaser, it was a peaceful period in Room Number 8, with no more bizarre events taking place. One night, Yaser even quipped that perhaps the room – or whoever was behind the incidents there and elsewhere in the hall – had felt sorry for them and decided to give them a chance to concentrate on their exams.

And because the first year was a preparatory one that emphasized English- and mathematics-enhancement modules for the new students, it was not hard for them to score well on their exams. Their achievements also gave them a great morale boost, and both were determined to reach the same high standards by putting in even more effort during the second term of the school year.

The holiday between the two terms also passed in the blink of an eye, and soon the two friends found themselves back at the door to Room Number 8, one day before classes resumed. Before they entered, they locked eyes for a moment, silently communicating the same question: *What awaits us inside?*

The only way to find out was to go in, so Yaser inserted his key into the lock, turned it, and pushed the door open, breaking the silence with a loud squeak. They peered inside, and even in darkness, they could sense that something was off; no specific expectations, just a shared suspicion that all was not well. Yusuf reached for the light switch and their suspicion was confirmed.

Chapter 33

The following day, Yusuf was walking from one campus building to another as he tried to make sense of what he and had found in the room. The place had been neat and tidy when they left, but what they returned to was total chaos. The chairs were upside down, the sheets and blankets from both beds lay in heaps on the floor, the wardrobe door was wide open, and most of the stuff on the shelves had been scattered elsewhere at random.

He recalled Yaser's initial response: "What a hellacious mess!" his friend had shouted.

The two of them had just stood there for a few minutes, stunned by the unpleasant spectacle. Then they had surrendered to reality and got down to the work of returning everything to its proper place and position. Although tidying up the room took considerable effort, and they were already tired from their trip, neither of them had slept well.

The next morning, they went straight to Ashraf to tell him what had happened. He told them that one of his friends from another housing block had experienced something similar: apparently, a cat had gotten into the guy's room and made quite a mess.

Neither Yaser nor Yusuf had put much stock in the cat theory at the time, but the more the latter thought about it, the more plausible it seemed. Perhaps one of those two cats, the ones that seemed to be invisible to everyone except him and Yaser, had somehow snuck into their room over the holidays and left before their return. It was possible, he decided, an estimation that briefly comforted him as he arrived at his next class.

Then another thought occurred to him. For the cat theory to be true, it meant that somewhere in the room was an opening big enough for an animal to pass through. *Now we have to find it.*

Chapter 34

That evening, as he waited for Yaser to return with supper, Yusuf performed a quick inspection of the room, looking for the spot that might have provided a secret entrance for a cat. All he found, however, were a few tiny cracks in one of the walls.

He was standing in the middle of the room, thinking of where he might look next, when he felt something on his leg. He saw nothing when he looked down, but then he felt it again, and this time he gasped slightly at the realization: something was moving on his left leg. Actually, he could feel several points of contact on his skin, so there was only one possible interpretation: some kind of creature was crawling on his leg – and it was inside the trousers of his tracksuit!

His heart skipped a beat. He had always been uncomfortable with insects and other creepy-crawlies, and the venomous ones were a particular fear. He swatted hard at the spot where the thing had last moved, but he must have missed because he felt the motion of its legs again, only this time it was higher up his leg. He tried repeatedly, and each time the thing crawled further up.

It was a childhood nightmare come true, and Yusuf decided that the only way to escape was to take the trousers off. He readied himself and pulled them down in one motion, still wondering what the thing was ... "A huge spider, human – with eight black legs and the deadliest venom!"

The sound of the terrible feminine voice coincided with several other alarming sensations. First it was intense numbness in his head, then the familiar pain under his chin, followed by a sudden headache so vicious that his eyes closed automatically and his hands came up to press on his temples. As excruciating as his physical pain was, he was even more troubled by what it meant: the demon's attacks were no longer limited to nightmares and night-time, but had extended to waking hours as well.

That frightful realization was immediately replaced by a more immediate one as he felt the texture of the little legs on his abdomen. He swatted at the spider through his jacket and the shirt underneath it, but again in vain as it dodged the blow.

"No! No!" Yusuf shouted as he felt it crawl around to his back.

Now he pulled off both the jacket and the shirt, tossing them side as his heart raced in morbid anticipation, dreading the moment when the spider would sink its fangs into him and inject its poison. Sweat covered most of his naked torso, and his heart beat like a jackhammer as he moved his hands madly on the skin of his belly, his chest, and the parts of his back he could reach. But he couldn't find it.

"Where did it go?" he asked out loud. "Where?!"

The only answer came from the dull buzz of the aging air conditioner. He thought the spider might have dropped down on the floor, so he looked down and started to spin around, trying desperately to spot it.

He barely completed a single rotation before he found its hiding place. He still couldn't see it, but he could feel it moving on his skin under the one piece of clothing he still had on – just below his waist.

Chapter 35

Yaser looked at his watch as he walked along the open corridor towards the room. He was carrying several bags of takeaway food for dinner and hoped his best friend would forgive him for being late.

The door was closed but not locked, which meant he did not have to fish for his keys, so he knocked lightly as a courtesy and, hearing nothing, walked inside crying: "Greetings ..."

He cut his cry very short and froze in place, taking in the scene before him with equal parts surprise and embarrassment.

Yusuf was standing in the middle of the room mostly naked, his clothes scattered on the floor around him. He was bathed in sweat and the expression on his face indicated only pain and confusion. Yaser had no idea what was going on, but he was deeply worried for his friend.

He went back to the door and locked it, then returned. He slowly approached his lifelong friend, gently shook his shoulder, and asked,

"Hey Yusuf, are you okay?"

Yusuf shuddered and muttered something unintelligible as the look of pain and confusion gave way to fear and something else: he looked at Yaser like he no longer recognized him. Yaser was really surprised at that, so he took a couple of steps backward, giving his friend space until he could ease him out of whatever he was going through.

"Take it easy, my friend," he said softly. "Nothing to worry about, it's me, Yaser. You want to tell me what happened here? Why are you standing in the middle of the room like this?"

Yusuf suddenly started looking around, as though he were seeing everything for the first time, then he appeared to regain awareness of where he was and what was going on. He seemed nervous, let out a long exhalation, and then started to collect his clothes from the floor as he finally answered:

"A strange insect managed to creep under my clothes, and you know how much I hate insects ... Now, please stop staring at me like that ... Thank you for bringing lunch ... Can you prepare the sheet whilst I get dressed?"

That answer was not nearly sufficient to satisfy Yaser's curiosity, but he had no desire to put pressure on his friend when he was in such a state. Instead, he tried to comfort his friend as he spread the plastic sheet on the floor to prepare for dinner. "I hate bugs too," he said, "and unfortunately the grassy area around our hall is filled with all sorts of them."

As was their habit during meal-times, they watched one of the few sports channels accessible by the TV's antenna because the satellite never worked. Every so often, Yaser took a quick look at his friend to check on him. Each time, Yusuf looked bewildered, and he barely touched the food.

Chapter 36

A couple of days later, Yusuf got back from his lectures and decided to take a shower. It tended to be less crowded at that time of the day, so he knew he would not have to wait for an empty stall. He put a change of clothes and some personal items in a plastic bag and headed down the corridor.

He quickly found and entered a vacant stall, shut the plastic curtain behind him, and was soon immersed in the warm falling water.

He took several deep breaths, trying to relax and let the water wash away the distress that burdened his heart and soul. So much was happening that he could not understand. Even the doctor at the university clinic had been no help, assuring him that he had no swelling or infection in his throat or tonsils, and nothing else that might have explained the recurring pain under his chin. Yusuf also wished that he could tell Yaser about the cruel female demon who had repeatedly assailed him, but he feared that it might damage their friendship, or even put his friend in danger.

When he was finished, he turned off the taps and started drying himself with a towel. He noticed that someone appeared to be waiting directly outside the stall; he could just make out the shape of a person through the shower curtain. He did not like to be rushed, especially when he knew there had to be other stalls available, so he called out sternly,

"Find another stall, brother. I'm still using this one."

There was no response, and the guy just kept standing there. It made no sense, and Yusuf started to feel impatient. He looked more carefully through the curtain to see if he could figure out who it was, but it was impossible to make out features. What he did notice, however, was unnerving: whoever it was, the outline of their body was not typically masculine. In fact, it was decidedly female! Now apprehension squeezed his gut as he recalled what had happened here at the beginning of the previous term, so he called out again, this time anxiously,

"Who's there?"

Again, his question received no reply, so he dressed quickly, not bothering to get completely dry. The pain under his chin made itself felt as his anxiety flared. He had not taken his eyes off the curtain, and now he steeled himself to go out. He pulled the curtain to the side, shouting,

"Why are you standing there ... "

The rest did not come out, for what he saw outside the stall froze him in his tracks.

Chapter 37

Yaser arrived at the housing block and was walking along the corridor towards the room when he saw a black cat coming out from the toilets and showers. It quickly crossed the small distance to the short wall that overlooked the green area in the middle of the building, jumped nimbly over it, and sank into the thick grass. The same moment, Yusuf popped his head out of the toilets section, looking up and down the corridor. As soon as he spotted his friend near their room, he hollered,

"Yaser, did you see it? The black cat?"

Yaser nodded and raised his voice to reply,

"Yes, I did. But it disappeared into the grass. You'll never catch it. Come back to the room."

One of the students in Room Number 14 peeked his head out the door and said teasingly, "Hey, guys, what's all the commotion? We can't study whilst you're exchanging cries in the corridor."

Yusuf crossed him on his way to his room and muttered, "Excuse me, Zuhair."

But Yaser replied to him laughingly, saying "Get back in your room, brother. I bet you were falling asleep anyway."

Zuhair's chubby body shook with a chuckle as he went back inside, closing his door behind him.

When Yusuf and Yaser got back to their room, the latter unloaded his books onto his desk and started changing his clothes.

Yusuf, however, was very agitated. He started pacing his side of the room like a caged animal. After a few laps, he angrily declared,

"I'm sick of this situation, Yaser. I can't bear it anymore!"

Yaser sat on his bed, leaned his back against the wall to face his friend, and asked,

"What happened this time?"

Yusuf kept pacing the room whilst he narrated the details of what had taken place in the showers, including the moment when he opened the curtain to find the black cat in front of him instead of the expected female, and the animal was staring at him, exactly as it had done the last time.

Yaser shook his head back and forth, saying,

"May God grant us refuge from Satan. Repeating the same scenario with the shadow and the cat cannot be a mere coincidence."

"Yes," Yusuf agreed, "and this is what bothers me and makes me lose my mind. I can't stand it anymore!"

Yaser retreated into his thoughts for awhile, whilst Yusuf sat at his desk and started reading one of his textbooks, trying to take his mind off what had taken place.

A little later, Yaser said, "I have a suggestion."

Yusuf turned towards him and asked, "What is it?"

"We could go live with Husam and Osama in their room for a couple of days, use the showers there, and see if these incidents happen again or not."

Yusuf conducted a quick mental analysis of the idea before objecting:

"I'm sorry, my friend, but I think that would be impractical. For one thing, how would we explain why we want to leave our room and go stay in theirs? For another, these incidents don't happen frequently or in any kind of pattern, which makes it impossible to define a time frame for how long we'd have to stay in their hall instead of here."

Yaser had to acknowledge that his friend was right.

"So what should we do?"

Yusuf had turned his eyes back to his book for a whole minute before he answered: "Let's see if we can find another room – in a hall far away from here – and move in there."

Yaser got off the bed and went to his own desk, letting out a deep sigh as he sat on the chair.

"Okay, let's try to visit Student Housing Affairs as soon as possible to discuss the issue with them," he said. "May God assist us."

Chapter 38

Several hours later, Yusuf was finally approaching sleep. He had been tossing and turning in his bed, and it was after midnight when he finally started to drift off. Then his eyes opened as a new sensation crept into his body, a tingling in the extremities combined with a slight chill, followed by a wave of quick pulses, as though from a weak electric current, that moved from top to toe. It brought comfort and happiness in a way he had never experienced before.

He did not understand what he was experiencing, so the questions started asking themselves. Was he still asleep and therefore dreaming? Or had he woken up? *And does that demon have anything to do with what I'm feeling?*

As if on cue, the answer came in a feminine voice, directly from inside his head.

"What do you think of what I am giving you this time, Yusuf?"

All symptoms of sleepiness were instantly gone. He had been focused on the ceiling in the faint light cast by a lamp in the corner, and when he tried to sit up and look around, nothing happened.

"Your body is still under my full control," the voice told him. "You will not be able to move."

It was true. He could not move. He could still feel, though, and it felt like something was perched on his chest. He could also think, and something occurred to him. "This is the first time you've used my name," he said, his voice quivering and barely audible. "It is also the first time I present you happiness instead of a headache and body pain, so which do you prefer?"

Her tone was different from before, too, taking some of the edge off his fear, so he answered with a question of his own:

"So I can choose how you exercise your power over me?"

"Yes, but this is the only choice I will give you."

The situation was very confusing, and Yusuf felt a little dizzy and short of breath. Then he remembered something.

"But what about the revenge that you were seeking?"

A seething hiss ensued, long and angry, throwing him back into abject terror. He closed his eyes and braced himself for the worst. But soon the hissing stopped, and the feminine voice in his head spoke with a mysterious softness.

"Do not remind me of getting revenge for my brother again. You will regret that forever if I return to seeking it."

Yusuf kept his eyes closed and asked another question:

"What do you want from me then?"

"To make a deal."

He felt all the astonishment in the universe.

"Ha! A deal? With me? How? And why?"

"After all this time I have spent inside your body, I have begun to feel things that I have never known before in my world. And I like what I have felt. For that reason, I wish to remain inside you for a longer period of time."

She appeared to have finished, but Yusuf did not answer right away. He held his tongue for a bit, trying to understand this new aspect of what he was facing. So he tried to learn more.

"You've entered my body without my permission," he recalled. "You've also repeatedly attacked me with pain and paralysis, and you can stay inside me even if I object. So on what basis shall we make a deal?!"

"There are things you can do which will maximize my pleasure whilst I am inside you. If you agree to provide those things, I will give you much more in return."

"And what if I refuse to cooperate with you?"

He still had his eyes closed, but now he clenched them tightly as the furious hissing returned:

"Then I will return to seeking revenge and retaliation, and you will receive nothing but pain and tribulation."

Point made, the voice softened again, regaining its soothing but mysterious femininity:

"And now, what is your decision?"

Yusuf thought of the two choices before him and quickly determined that agreeing to the deal would be far better than refusing it

"Okay, I agree to allow you to stay in my body and to help you, but what should I call you?"

"You shall call me 'Habiba.'"

Yusuf thought this more than a little ironic, considering that she had selected a name that was also a term of endearment meaning "beloved."

"'Habiba?'" he whispered "What an extraordinary use of the name!"

"And now," she said, "open your eyes."

Yusuf complied instantly – and was astounded by the beauty of what he saw!

Chapter 39

After Yusuf woke up the next morning, he stayed in bed for a while, relaxing as he thought about what had transpired a few hours earlier. It had been a long time since he had felt so content.

He was still marvelling at how quickly his situation had changed, especially given all the terror and apprehension that had grown inside him since that night on the ground floor of his family's house in Makkah. After several confrontations with Habiba, all of which were accompanied by pain and trepidation, here he was, experiencing levels and calm and happiness that he had not previously known to exist. The feeling was so special that it compensated for the disturbing fact that his female interlocutor was indeed a demon, not a mere figment of nightmares or hallucinations as he had previously thought.

He took a deep breath and popped out of bed with new energy. When he noticed that Yaser's bed was empty, he spoke to himself out loud: "Wow! This is the first time he's left the room without waking me up!"

Then he looked at the alarm clock, slowly realizing what happened, and some of his ebullience evaporated.

"How could this have happened?" he asked himself. He picked up the clock to look it at more closely and make sure he was seeing the time correctly.

He was. "It's ten o'clock in the morning! How could I

have not heard the alarm? I'll miss the manufacturing skills lab. God!"

He tossed the alarm clock onto his bed, dressed as quickly as he could, grabbed the books and other materials he needed, and ran out to his car. By the time he pulled into the parking lot next to the preparatory-year labs, he had broken into an anxious sweat. This was his first time being late for any lecture or laboratory session at university, and the idea of losing his perfect attendance record caused him real aggravation.

When he reached the door to the lab, he stopped to take a deep breath, filling his lungs with the building's cool air. Then he exhaled slowly, trying to dissipate some of his stress. He looked at his wrist watch, which informed him that half of the session had already passed.

Both the students and the lab supervisor – a European who spoke little or no Arabic and was known for coming down hard on anyone who failed to meet his expectations – went silent as soon as Yusuf entered sheepishly. The looks directed at him range from surprise and pity to mockery and resentment.

"Good morning, Mr. John. I'm very sorry for being late," he managed to say. The supervisor lived up to his reputation, remarking, "Look who has honoured us with his gracious presence, and just like any eminent personality: fashionably late."

Some of the students laughed at that, but Yusuf felt bullied and humiliated. He continued towards the table that held his project, an in-progress metal box, and felt compelled to defend himself: "Again, I apologize, but this my first time being late all year, and I didn't do it on purpose."

"Apologize as much as you like, but it changes nothing. Your name has been recorded in the list of absentees for today's lab. Now go ahead, keep working on that ugly box."

Some of the students laughed again before everyone went back to working on their boxes. Yusuf got to work too, but inside he was livid at the supervisor for having mocked and belittled him. Even the pain under his chin flared. He managed to control his expression so as not to betray the resentment he felt, but his mind had only desire, something he had never imagined before.

Ever.

Chapter 40

Before Yaser went back to the room, he visited the Student Housing Affairs office to investigate the possibility of getting himself and Yusuf transferred to another residence block.

The clerk he dealt with said he could look into it and brought up the necessary information on his screen. Then he frowned.

"But it's only been a few months since you were assigned the room," he said.

"And what's the problem with that?" Yaser asked.

"The housing rules state that a student cannot change their room before two years have elapsed since it was assigned. And after this period, there have to be other students who wish to move out to make a switch possible."

Yaser's shoulders sank when he realized that this process might be much more difficult than he had suspected, but he did not give up.

"What if we found two students from a different hall who are willing to swap now? Then would you be able to help us?"

The man shook his head, so Yaser pressed on, insisting, "Please, sir. The situation is very difficult in that room. We really need to move."

"Why? What is the nature of the hardship that necessitates an urgent change?"

"I can't give you the details. There are very personal issues involved."

"Forgive me, son, but the instructions are clear and the monitoring of their application is very strict. May God pave your way."

Yaser sighed in surrender, thanked the clerk for his time, and left. He crossed the short distance between it and the housing block absentmindedly, but once he saw it, he felt like the building was laughing at him because he and his friend had failed to escape its grasp.

Chapter 41

"The attempt to change halls has failed miserably," Yaser said that evening as he tried to find something to watch on television.

Yusuf raised his head from the novel he was reading and looked at his best friend, saying, "So you had the chance to visit the housing office today. Thanks for that, but what happened? Why did it fail?"

Yaser relayed what the clerk had told him in the afternoon. Yusuf sighed as he looked around the room before commenting.

"It seems this room will not allow us to leave it," he said.

Yaser shared his thoughts, saying, "I feel deep distress in my chest. Instead of students in Room Number 8, it's like we're prisoners in Cell Number 8!"

Just then someone knocked on the door. It was unlocked, so Yusuf shouted, "Come in, please!"

Husam opened the door and walked inside.

"Hey guys, is this a convenient time?"

Yusuf and Yaser remembered their manners and got up to greet him, and soon they were chatting about their studies and the difficulty of living under so many different rules and systems. Husam sensed that something was bothering them, so he made a suggestion.

"I forgot to tell you about the Friends List service," he said. "It can be fun, and offers some practical benefits too."

It was Yusuf who responded: "Friends List? What's that?"

"It's a service the university provides for both teachers and students. It's based on the idea of connecting the mainframe computer to the internet using what's called a 'relay chat' and…"

Husam could tell from their expressions that they had no idea what he was talking about, so he chuckled a bit, adjusted his glasses, and continued with a different approach.

"I won't bore you with the technical details. What I mean to say is that those who subscribe to the Friends List can communicate with all the other subscribers in an open space for discussions, information sharing, cultural exchanges, just about anything about any subject."

His brother asked, "And how can we join?"

"There's a special lab at the FIT Building – that's the Faculty of Information Technology – where they have computer devices that are connected to the internet. This is the only way to use the service, and because most of the list users are in Western countries, you have to consider the time difference. A lot of times, it means you have to be there at night."

Yusuf was curious about the last point, so he asked another question: "Doesn't the university lock its doors at night?"

"Most of them are locked, but there are some doors are left open so professors and lecturers can use their offices whenever they want, and the same goes for this lab as well. The buildings all have security guards around the clock anyway."

Yaser was sceptical.

"Why are you asking all these questions, Yusuf? Do you really want to waste your time on this Friends List?"

Yusuf shrugged his shoulders, saying, "It's not like I'm committing to anything right now, but knowing how to join can't do any harm, can it?"

Husam looked at Yaser and said, "It seems that the service has not captured your imagination, my friend!"

"Man, I've got enough with the long hours I spend every day at university to attend lectures and labs," Yaser replied. "I don't want to even think of returning there in the evening."

Husam nodded his head in understanding, whilst Yusuf smiled and quipped, "The nights and soirées ... "

Yaser laughed the comment, and Husam was gladdened by the harmony between his brother and his friend. Then he looked at his watch and said it was time to go. He got up to leave but stopped just as he opened the door.

"Hey," he said. "Where's the mirror that was jammed between the shelves?"

Yusuf and Yaser exchanged a quick glance before the former answered with a nervous laugh.

"It fell and shattered," he told his brother. "It seems that it couldn't bear being stuck in one place any longer!"

Chapter 42

Later, the two roommates were in their respective beds, almost ready for sleep. At the same time, a small creature moved quickly but quietly across the floor, heading straight for one of the wooden legs at the foot of Yaser's bed. The young man's upper body was propped up in one of the corners where the head of his bed met the wall, a pillow behind him for support, but his mind was in another world, courtesy of the novel he was reading.

The creature got closer and closer to its target, reaching the leg closest to Yaser's foot and then climbing deftly until it was on the mattress. Now the wicked little thing was just a few steps away, its intended victim still engrossed in his book as it made its final approach.

Before it got there, the creature's movement caught Yusuf's eye, causing him instinctively to shift his gaze in that direction. As soon as his focus sharpened, he recognized the threat and shouted,

"Yaser! Look out!"

Yaser flinched at the warning, sitting up a little straighter and yelling, "What? What happened?"

Before there was time for an answer, the problem was readily apparent. His new position allowed him to see the small but deadly creature approaching him, so he quickly withdrew both of his legs and folded them underneath him. But he was still trapped in the corner formed by the wall and the headboard, frozen in fear. He started screaming.

"A scorpion! On my bed! Yusuf, do something!"

Yusuf was terrified too. His phobia about all things venomous was in high gear, and he cringed at the realization that the scorpion could just as easily have crawled into his own bed. But his best friend was in danger: he forced himself out of bed and onto the floor, crossing to Yaser's side of the room and wondering what to do. As for the scorpion, its eight little legs carried its shiny black body ever closer to Yaser, its nerve-wracking approach all the more horrifying for how cruelly slow it was.

Even at that pace, there was no more time for delay, but Yusuf could go no further. He was paralyzed by fear.

It was Yaser who finally noticed the stack of books on his desk, just within reach. A rush of adrenaline rising inside him, he grabbed the biggest hard-cover in the stack, then – stretching his arm to its maximum length – used it to knock the scorpion onto the floor. The thing tried to scuttle away, but just as it reached the rug next to his bed, Yaser let out a savage roar and threw the massive tome on top of the hideous creature.

Then all was silent except for the familiar buzz of the air conditioner. Several moments passed before Yusuf snapped out of his torpor

"Is everything over?" he asked.

Yaser took a deep breath to calm down and glanced around all four corners of the room saying, "Well, there's no way for any scorpion to survive getting hit with that much weight on a solid floor. But that's not what worries me now. The real question is: How did it get in here? And are there any more?"

ROOM NUMBER 8

They immediately started searching the room but were soon interrupted by several loud knocks on the door. "Come in!" they both shouted.

It was Ashraf. "Hey, guys," he said. "What's going on in here? I heard screams and a crash."

Yusuf quickly told him what had happened, and Ashraf headed straight to where the book lay on the floor. Yusuf and Yaser watched in morbid fascination as he carefully lifted it up, just enough to see underneath. Once he was sure it was dead, he turned the book over and left it on the floor.

"Yuck," Ashraf said. "How disgusting."

Yusuf asked, "How will we clean the rug?"

Then it was Yaser's turn: "My book is no longer fit for human consumption!"

The scorpion had mostly been split into two parts. One was stuck to the cover of the book, whilst the other was smeared into the fabric of the rug, with the two pieces still linked by a few gooey threads.

"I've never heard of a scorpion showing up in someone's room in this hall," Ashraf said, "but there's a first time for everything. Thank God you're safe."

With that, he gathered up the remains of the scorpion in a bag and carried it out to the dumpster in the street. Then he came back and helped clean the rug.

Chapter 43

That night was one of the worst Yusuf and Yaser had ever lived. Their encounter with the scorpion – not just within what we all imagine to be the safety of home, but right up on one of their beds – left them deeply shaken and highly paranoid. They resisted sleep so they could watch the corners of the room to make sure no more scorpions (or snakes, for that matter) could creep in unnoticed and attack them as they dreamed. At first they chatted to pass the time. Then they took shifts, one on guard and the other trying to get some rest, and so it went until the dawn of the next day.

As the time of their first lectures approached, they started the day both anxiously and groggily, their steps unsteady and their eyelids heavy due to lack of sleep.

As he drove to class, Yusuf cursed the scorpion, which had not only deprived both them of a night's sleep but had also denied him, in particular, the meeting he had expected with Habiba.

The thought had barely formed in his mind when he started to question it. Now his hatred for the scorpion was replaced by surprise and then self-condemnation over having had such thoughts about a demon. *I used to pray that she would stay away, and now I'm sad because she didn't show up. How did that happen?!*

Such were the questions rolling around in his mind as he entered the building that held the preparatory-year classrooms, but his focus soon changed as he got involved in his studies and discussions with fellow students.

Then one of them mentioned the manufacturing lab, and someone else quickly interjected, "Did you hear the latest about Mr. John?"

Yusuf's senses had been dulled by the difficult night, but now he was fully alert, listening carefully to what the others were saying about the lab supervisor who had embarrassed him in front of the whole class. Another student replied, "I did hear something about him, but I can't vouch for the accuracy of the information, and I don't like to spread rumours."

Yusuf suddenly snapped, "Stop beating around the bush and get to the point! What's the news about him?"

The student who had raised the matter gave him a very serious look as he answered, "They say he had a terrible car accident."

Another third student cried, "Oh! How awful."

Yusuf muttered, almost under his breath, "But ... did he die?"

"No, and they say it's a miracle that he survived, but he's liable to end up wishing for death every second rather than living with intense pains and permanent impairment."

"There is no power and no strength except with Allah," the second student commented.

"His condition sounds heartbreaking."

Yusuf withdrew from the discussion with contradictory feelings. He could not decide whether he should feel sympathy for the unfortunate supervisor – or satisfaction because this sort of thing was pretty much what he had wished for the previous day, after the man had given him such a hard time for having been late.

It bothered him that he felt such confusion, and he went to the next lecture with a distracted mind.

Chapter 44

That evening, Yusuf and Yaser felt like a century had passed since they last slept, so they had a light dinner and got ready for an early night. Yusuf turned off the big white bulbs that flooded the room with light, leaving only single small lamp on as they fell into their respective beds.

Yaser yawned hard, then said, "We have to sleep very deeply tonight, even if the world's entire population of scorpions decides to visit us."

An exhausted Yusuf laughed sleepily, commenting, "If all the scorpions of the world had attacked us, we would've slept forever."

When he spoke again, his tone was more serious.

"I don't think I'll ever have a deep or comfortable sleep in this room again," he said. "My sense of security was gone after that critter showed up."

Then he asked: "Did you hear what happened to Mr. John?"

"Supervisor John? Please don't remind me ... absolutely silly and arrogant ... What happened to him?"

Yusuf told him the news he had heard from the other students that afternoon, then confessed how much hatred and resentment he had carried in his heart after the supervisor had mocked him the previous morning. He even admitted to having wished he had the ability to cause the man the worst possible pain.

Yaser paused for a moment, then replied: "I'm surprised

to hear you had such negative and violent emotions inside you. I've always known you to be calm and forgiving, ever since childhood."

Yusuf looked at the ceiling and sighed deeply.

"Believe me," he said. "I'm even more surprised!"

Yaser closed his eyes and his tongue sounded heavy when he said, "Anyway, we'll have nothing more to do with him now. Good night."

"Good night."

Within minutes, they were both fast asleep.

Chapter 45

It was after midnight and Yusuf was still sleeping deeply when his left hand moved up and his fingers started tickling the skin under his chin. Within a few minutes, the sequence had pulled Yusuf out of his slumber and into a state of vigilance. His eyes stayed shut as he murmured quietly, "My chin! What's happening?!"

He lay on his on his belly and was surprised to realize that through no effort his own, his fingers continued to tickle the skin under his chin unconsciously.

"It is I, Yusuf."

All his senses were alerted by those words – more specifically, by the soft feminine voice that generated them from inside his head. He instantly opened his eyes and noted the faint light supplied by the small lamp. He tried to move his head so he could look around, but to no avail. When he spoke, his voice carried both yearning and concern.

"Hello, Habiba."

"Were you pleased with what I did for you?"

"What do you mean?" he asked. "What did you do?"

Her voice firmed up. Now it was impatient, a little angry: "Do you really have no idea, or are you pretending, human?"

"Believe me, Habiba, I don't understand what you're talking about!"

She returned to a softer femininity, but still a cunning one.

"That wretch who intended to hurt your feeling two days ago."

His heartbeat accelerated at her words. With a supreme effort, he managed to pull his fingers a few millimetres away from that spot under his chin.

Then he asked, "Do you mean John, the lab supervisor?"

"Yes, that miserable fool."

"Oh! What did you do to him?"

"I made your wish come true. I took your revenge"

"What? How? Tell me."

A strong chill hit his back and neck, then an increase in pressure on them, and he sensed both pride and power as Habiba hissed inside his head:

"I left your body when you unleashed your desire to hurt him, and I watched that wretch until the suitable time came. Then I appeared before his car in my most horrific form. It only took a second. And now here I am back in your body, where my comfort and pleasure are."

Yusuf closed his eyes and took a deep breath, trying to control his reaction and resolve his dilemma. Would he sympathize with the human tragedy that had struck John and his family? Or would he rejoice with Habiba at what she had done for him?

The latter realized what was going on inside his mind, so she exercised the power she had over his body: small vibrations, very much like electric pulses, reached every part of his body Yusuf smiled as he focused on getting as much comfort and happiness as he could from the sensation.

Then, his voice calm and relaxed, he asked,

"But how do you get out of my body and return again without me noticing? That first time, in Makkah, was very rough and clear."

Habiba's laugh sounded like the ringing of tens of brass

bells. Then she spoke, her voice feminine voice laden with both sweetness and mystery.

"The first entry to your body had to be done in a special and unique way," she explained, "but do not concern yourself with this. I have vast capabilities that are beyond your comprehension. Now, go back to sleep."

In seconds, as though he had been waiting only for her to give the order, Yusuf was immersed again in the seas of sleep.

Chapter 46

When Yusuf woke to the sound of the alarm clock in the morning, he adjusted his position on his bed and took a quick look at Yaser, who was still asleep. Then he took a moment to enjoy the pleasure of the new inner feeling that filled his body, a sensation that revolved around a single word: power!

Now Habiba resided inside him, with all her "vast capabilities" and her evident willingness to promptly retaliate against anyone who crossed him, he was in a position of rare privilege. *In fact,* he thought, I *might be the only person on earth who wields such power.*

He jumped up from his bed and imagined that his muscles had puffed up a little bit, so he pulled off his shirt and posed in front of their long mirror. He was sure his muscles had not changed one bit, but he smiled at his reflection anyway.

Then he went out in the corridor and started moving back and forth between the room and the toilets, all the while humming a recent pop song. This was when Yaser woke up, but as soon as he saw what was happening, he had doubts.

"Am I dreaming?" he asked when Yusuf returned to the room. "Or is my best friend really that happy being up so early to prepare for a stinking class?"

Yusuf laughed, then smiled and winked at his friend as he finished getting dressed. "Hey Yaser. Everything has a beginning ... and this is my beginning with joy."

He paused for a moment before adding:

"And power!"

Yaser had no idea what his friend was referring to, so he watched in silence until Yusuf finished all his preparations and headed out of the room crying, "See you later, my friend!"

Once Yusuf had left, Yaser just sat there staring at the door for awhile, the surrounding quiet only magnifying the enormity of the question in his mind:

What on earth could have happened to make him change like that, literally overnight?

Chapter 47

"Wow! A new stereo! Excellent!"

Yusuf was thrilled when he saw his best friend enter the room with the device that evening. Yaser closed the door behind him and headed towards his half of the room, then unloaded the box he was carrying onto his desk, saying,

"Good evening, roommate. How are you? I would like to clarify that we will be using this device for one purpose only."

"And what is that?"

"For playing the Surat Al-Baqarah when we're away from the room from time to time."

Yusuf's features transformed from rejoice to puzzlement. Al-Baqarah was the longest surah in the Quran, a listing of basic rules regarding everything from agriculture and the banning of usury to the proper treatment of orphans and a call for Jews and Christians to accept the Prophet Mohammed.

"Surat Al-Baqarah? Why?"

Yaser answered as he was changing his clothes,

"Man, you know how much strange stuff has happened since our arrival here ... My mother says this will help bring good luck, so let's try and see if ... "

His words stopped dead at the sound. He stood stock-still, trying to ignore the thumping in his chest as he waited to see if he would hear it again. Yusuf was stiff as a board, too, and they were both staring at the same spot: the main door of the big wardrobe against the wall.

Without taking his eyes off the door, Yaser asked, "Did you hear that?"

His friend answered slowly, "Yes, I did, very clearly, but what could it be?"

The sound returned, and it was definitely coming from inside the wardrobe. They struggled to understand what it could be this time. Then the noise got louder as whatever was inside the closet started hurling itself against the side walls and the heavy main door!

"Perhaps it's a cat again," Yaser suggested.

"How could it have got in there? The door to the room is always shut, and so is the wardrobe!"

Neither of them had an answer, and both were already on edge after all the inexplicable events they had experienced since having arrived on campus. The noise inside the wardrobe was not only getting louder, but also becoming more insistent too, like something was determined to break free and attack them. The two young men grew increasingly fearful, and Yaser shouted a prayer:

"I seek refuge in God from Satan. May God protect us!"

Chapter 48

Ashraf was sitting at his desk, trying to finish an assignment, when he heard the first noises from the other side of the wall he shared with Room Number Eight. He frowned as he put his ear to the wall, recalling some of the painful events that place had witnessed in the past. He quickly set such musings aside, however, instead wondering: *Are the guys trying to do some renovations in their wardrobe?*

He sat back down on his chair and tried to focus on getting his work done, but immediately the noise got worse. He headed into the corridor and with just a couple of steps, he crossed the distance to his neighbours' door. He knocked quietly, not wanting to betray his impatience at the interruption.

There was no answer, and he could hear the commotion inside growing more intense. Now Ashraf was getting a little excited, too. He knocked on the door again, harder this time, and yelled,

"Yaser! Yusuf! What's going on?"

He heard the sound of the lock sliding, so he pushed the door open and entered the room, which was a half-step higher than the level of the floor in the corridor. As soon as he saw what was happening, his eyes widened and his feet automatically carried him backward.

The moment Ashraf entered the room, he saw the heavy wooden door of the wardrobe separate violently from its frame and fall towards Yaser, who cried out as he raised his arms to protect his head and barely got out of the way in time. The solid-wood door hit the rock-hard floor with a resounding crash that echoed off the walls of the small room, then resonated far down the corridor.

For a few seconds, the only sound in the room was that of the rickety air conditioner. Then came voices from the corridor; it sounded like everyone in their hall had heard the noise and wanted to know what had happened. Ashraf walked further into the room, asking,

"Are you guys okay?"

He found Yusuf cringing next to the bed nearest the door, apparently unable to speak, whilst Yaser was staring intently into the open wardrobe. Then Yaser grabbed the box with the new stereo in it off the desk and moved purposefully towards the wardrobe, raising the box above his head.

Ashraf shouted, "Yaser! What are you doing?"

But there was no stopping Yaser at that point. He threw the box down violently on top of the creature, which had no chance to escape. Such was the force of the blow that several sounds got mixed together, including the dull thud of the box hitting the floor of the wardrobe, the unmistakeable tinkle of electronic components shattering, an audible splat, and what sounded like bones breaking. Then, apart from the AC, it was quiet again.

Yaser did his best to regain control of his emotions as he kept his eyes on the box in the wardrobe. Ashraf came over and gave him a pat on the shoulder.

Still breathing heavy, and still focused on the box, Yaser said, "Thank God for your safety. It was God's mercy that protected me from that door."

Ashraf agreed with a nod of his head before turning to examine the wardrobe.

"How did the door collapse?" he asked. "And what did you hit with the box?"

"I have no idea about the door, but I saw a big rodent, probably a rat."

"Oh my only God!" Ashraf exclaimed. "Scorpions, rats ... What is it with you and gross animals?"

The question hung in the air as Ashraf stepped towards the wardrobe for a closer inspection.

"Hmm, the hinges look a little worn out, but was that enough for the door to collapse?"

Yusuf finally murmured something from his spot on the bed, where he was sitting with his knees pulled into his chest and his fingers nervously scratching the skin under his chin: "Another strange incident after the teapot and the mirror."

Yaser finally laid his hands on the box to move it off the flattened corpse underneath, and the three of them cleaned up the mess. Long after they were done, though, something still bothered him. Deep inside, he wondered about the nature of the sudden, irresistible urge that had caused him to smash the stereo, in particular, with his own hands:

Of all the objects I could've used to kill that thing, why did I pick the one that was brand-new?

Chapter 49

As had happened after the scorpion incident, Yusuf and Yaser scarcely slept at all that night. Both of them woke up the next morning with weary bodies and fretful souls, heading off to their classes in the same dreary mood.

As Yusuf approached the dorm at the end of the day, he remembered that before they went to bed, he had Yaser had discussed the need for one of them to visit the housing office; the damage needed to be reported, and they had to submit a maintenance request for the wardrobe door. He also remembered that it was his turn to go there, so he changed course and walked over.

As expected, the news of the fallen door came as quite a surprise to the clerk, and Yusuf could not miss the glance of suspicion directed at him. Having no logical explanation for what happened, he ignored the unspoken accusation.

Afterward, he paused before entering his room, feeling very much like he used to at the door to the ground floor of his family's house in Makkah, and whispered: "What's your story, Room Number 8? And what else have you got in store for us?"

Only silence answered him, so he took a deep breath, unlocked the door, and went inside, closing the door behind him. He put his books and a few other things on his desk, then looked towards the corner where the long mirror was. He felt drawn to it, so he went over and took a long look at his reflection. Suddenly, he felt itchy under his chin. He had been scratching at the spot for some time when he heard Habiba's voice inside his head.

"Yusuf, are you happy about what I did for you?"

He felt goose-bumps rising, as well as a twinge of fear mixed with a happy sense of anticipation. Eyes still on the mirror, fingers still scratching under his chin, he asked quietly,

"Were ... you ... the one who sabotaged the wardrobe door?""

The laugh still sounded like a snake, and its mysterious tone was an unsolvable riddle, but he nonetheless felt a wave of pleasure and happiness. Then he heard her say,

"No, I am not the one who did that."

"What have you done then? I don't understand you."

"Your friend," she began.

"Yaser? What about him? Come on, tell me!"

Now her voice exuded vanity and power: "I made him smash that device with his own hands, without him even knowing it."

Yusuf thought for a moment, searching his memory for the details of the previous night's events to make sure he understood things correctly. Then he smiled, saying, "Indeed, it really bothered me when he told me why he bought it, but I didn't expect such a quick reaction from you!"

"You will not be able to predict all of my actions, Yusuf ... Now, I want you to do something for me, for my pleasure."

"Sure, Habiba. Tell me what to do."

She did not need to speak inside his head, as he had already started doing what she wanted.

Chapter 50

When Yaser returned to the room after he had finished his classes for the day, he found the door locked, which usually meant that his friend was still out, so he did not bother to knock. He took out his key and was soon inside, closing the door behind him.

It had been long day after a mostly sleepless night, and he sighed as he threw his books and notes on his desk. He started to change his clothes but stopped immediately when he heard something. It came and went almost instantly, so he could not identify the sound or exactly where it had come from, but it was close. He listened carefully for a few seconds, then quickly finished changing, holding his breath to make sure he could hear anything out of place.

Not hearing anything else, he chalked it up to frayed nerves and lay down on the bed, stretching muscles that had got too little rest the previous night, then got stiff from long hours of sitting in lectures and labs all day. He wondered where Yusuf was, then began to reflect on the changes he had begun to notice in his friend. He resolved to discuss the matter with him so they could figure out the problem and try to resolve it.

The mysterious sound suddenly returned, yanking him out of his thoughts, but it lasted less than a second, just like the first time. This time, however, he thought he had located the place where the sound had come from: somewhere near Yusuf's bed.

ROOM NUMBER 8

Tension engulfed Yaser as he sat up in his own bed, directing all his focus at the other side of the room as he looked for what could have made the sounds he had heard. Seeing nothing on Yusuf's bed or on the floor next to it, he stopped to think, and it was like a light came on in his brain: *beneath* Yusuf's bed. It was semi-dark and hard to see under there, he thought to himself, but that would explain why he had not found what he was looking for. *That must be where it's coming from!*

Yaser got up and looked around for an implement to help in his little expedition, his eyes soon falling on his huge maths textbook. He retrieved it from his desk and took a few hesitant steps towards his friend's bed, then got down on his knees. He still had to get down even lower, almost prostrating himself, to see what awaited him under the bed, and that would make him vulnerable if something jumped out at him. Gathering his courage, he hefted the book in his hand, uttered a near-silent appeal to God, and put his hands on the floor so he could handle the weight shift.

Just as he reached the point where his line of sight would be unobstructed, a voice rang out, very close-by: "Wait! Yaser, don't look!"

Yaser almost jumped out of his skin.

Chapter 51

Two maintenance workers moved slowly down the corridor of the housing block, their pace limited by the heavy wardrobe door they carried, whilst a third leisurely led the way with a metal toolbox swinging from his hand.

Once they reached Room Number 8, one of them knocked on the door several times, then following up with their standard announcement: "Room maintenance! May we come in?"

Like their counterparts everywhere, the maintenance men hoped no one was home. They had a master key to let themselves in with, and it was easier to get their work done without anyone in the way. Nonetheless, they followed policy and allowed ample time for a response, having no way of knowing what was unfolding inside.

Just then, Yaser was crawling away from his friend's bed. He caught a quick glimpse of something, but could not identify what part of Yusuf's body it could possibly be.

"Yusuf! What is that? You scared me ... What are you doing under the bed?!"

His friend replied quietly, "It's not important what I'm doing ... The important thing is not to see me."

"I don't understand! Why don't you want me to see you?"

"Because I'm completely naked."

Yaser's eyes widened and his eyebrows seemed to climb half-way up his forehead.

"What?! Are you crazy? Why would you cram yourself naked into such a tight space?!"

Increasingly impatient with the questions, Yusuf spoke as quickly as he could: "This is not the time for arguing and insults. The maintenance guys are going to come in any second if we don't answer them. Please, go to the door right now and try to distract so I can put on my clothes. We can't let them get in here whilst I'm in this situation."

Yaser was deeply curious and just as concerned about what was going on with his friend, but Yusuf was right: he really had to delay the workers to keep things from getting worse.

"You're right," he said, quickly standing up and smoothing his clothes.

A moment later, he was standing in the corridor talking to the maintenance crew, giving Yusuf the time he needed to get out from under the bed and put some clothes on.

Chapter 52

Once the maintenance crew had finished installing the new wardrobe door, Yaser signed the receipt to close the request and thanked them for their efforts as he showed them out. He went to his desk, grabbed his chair, and placed it near Yusuf's bed. He took and released a deep breath as he sat down, his eyes focused on his lifelong friend, who was sitting on his bed in that horizontal way that they both preferred.

"Now, tell me about everything, please ... I want to understand."

Yusuf avoided eye contact, murmuring, "There isn't much to tell."

"Yusuf, I'm your best friend, the one you can trust most after your parents, and I've noticed some changes in you in recent days, but I don't know why."

Yusuf looked around the room, clearly hesitant to speak, so Yaser continued:

"I think it started when I came home that evening to find you standing almost naked in the middle of the room. Shortly thereafter, I opened my eyes one morning and you were showing off your chest in the mirror, then you went singing down the corridor. There's also that weird way you're always scratching under your chin. And today you really freaked me out by being naked under the bed. Only God knows what you might do next! So please, what's this all about? Tell me. What's going on with you?"

Yusuf finally answered but remained evasive. "Yaser, don't

complicate the simple things," he said. "It's just a childish behaviour from time to time. I see no harm in this."

"Childish behaviour? You call all this childish behaviour? Man, I feel like I don't know you anymore!"

Yaser had shouted those words. Now he lowered his head, shook it back and forth, and added sorrowfully, "Yes, for the first time in our long years of friendship, I that's how I feel. There is something different in you, but I don't know what it is."

Yusuf tried to put his mind at ease, saying, "It's okay my friend. Perhaps I really am going through some swings and slight changes, but my heart and the love and friendship it carries for you haven't changed. Don't worry."

"I'm not worried about our friendship, but about you and your safety."

A mysterious smile crossed Yusuf's lips and his reply was no less cryptic.

"From this side, don't worry about me at all," he said. "My power has vastly increased."

Yaser could not help but feel that his discussion with his friend had been counterproductive. Instead of getting an explanation from him, he had received only added mystery and deeper confusion. As a result, he was now more concerned than ever.

Chapter 53

A few days later, Yusuf parked near a group of buildings that housed several university faculties and other sections, including the Faculty of Information Technology. It was well past ten o'clock at night, so the parking lot was completely empty as he stepped down and looked up with apprehension at the group of mostly darkened structures before him. Earlier that day, he had decided to subscribe to the Friends List service. He thought it might help him find other people who had had experiences similar to his with Habiba. As he was walked slowly towards the FIT building, he did a mental review of what Husam had told him about which door was left open at night and how to join the list.

When he reached the right door, Yusuf turned to look if anyone else happened to be around, whether it was a student, a professor, or a security guard, but he saw no one. He felt nervous and his throat was dry, so he swallowed a little saliva. Then he tried the door handle. It worked, the door opened with only a little pressure, and he entered the building. He felt an instant chill as the cold air of the central air conditioning system hit him, but it dissipated when he closed the door, eliminating the pressure difference.

Whoever visits a building at night, in silence and with very little light to see by, would be blown away to experience how busy and crowded it gets during the day. That was what occurred to Yusuf as he walked the corridors searching for the computer lab. His brother had said it would be easy to find because it was surrounded by huge clear-glass windows running along the upper portions of all four walls surrounding it.

Sure enough, Yusuf found it very quickly and went inside. He settled in at one of the terminals, and within minutes had completed the Friends List registration process. Messages from subscribers about their various subjects started appearing on the screen in English, and Yusuf was excited to make such quick progress, spending nearly half an hour reading various posts and getting acquainted with the system.

Then he started asking about the subject of demons and confrontations between them and the humans. He was not expecting much of a response, but much to his surprise, the replies from other subscribers poured in quickly. Some members used their messages to recount the details of actual experiences, whilst others expressed opinions or shared general knowledge about the subject. There was plenty of information, and Yusuf had been going through it for about an hour when the silence of the place was disrupted by a loud noise.

It was right around midnight when he heard it, and although he could not be sure, he thought it sounded like a slamming door. He shivered a bit, then started turning around to look out into the surrounding corridors, hoping to see what had caused the noise.

He soon got his wish as a man suddenly appeared through the glass and made his way down one side of the lab. The position of the windows allowed Yusuf to see the man's head and torso, but the low light prevented him from distinguishing any features. He figured it was one of the professors, and that made him nervous because he might have to answer questions about what he was doing there so late. It was a pleasant surprise, then, when the man totally ignored him as he passed outside the lab and headed into one of the side corridors.

Almost unconsciously, Yusuf got up and moved towards the door, hoping to see which way the man was going. As soon as he got to the door, he stuck his head out and looked down the corridor. What he saw made him close his eyes and shake his head to make sure his vision wasn't blurred. He looked again, just in time to see the many go around a corner and out of sight. The windows had only let him see the man's upper body, but once he was out in the corridor and had a full floor-to-ceiling view, he noticed something very, very peculiar.

Yusuf was still unsure of what he had seen, wondering if maybe the weak lighting was playing tricks with his vision.

Is that what it was? Or was that guy really just floating along with no legs?

Chapter 54

Back in the room, Yaser had finished studying for a test the following day. Now he lay in bed on his back, fingers laced behind his head as he stared at the ceiling and returned to one of his many recent concerns.

He was still wondering about the force that had propelled him to smash the new stereo by throwing it on the rat, even though he had known – in the moment – that it was the wrong course of action. Why had he not been able to respond to his own objections and control his actions? *I knew I should find something – anything – else to kill it with, so why didn't I?*

The main reason for Yaser's distress was neither the destruction of the device nor the money wasted as a result, but rather the implicit truth that it was not the first time he had lost control over his behaviour and decision-making in a decisive moment. It had had happened on at least two or three other occasions, and he wondered if that constituted a pattern and, if so, might it indicate that he was suffering from some form of mental illness? He worried about his future if he could no longer trust himself to act rationally.

Suddenly, the door flew open violently. Yaser released a quick cry of surprised as he jumped to his feet, expecting whoever had thrown the door open like that to enter the room.

But no one came in.

Yaser stretched his neck to see better into the corridor from his position near the bed, but he saw no one near the doorway.

"Who's there?" he shouted.

There was only silence, so he walked towards the door to see if he could figure out what was going on. His heart beat rapidly as he crossed the short distance to the doorway, not knowing what to expect. When he got there, he looked both ways down the corridor. There was no one there.

At least, there was no one he could see.

Chapter 55

Yusuf rubbed his eyes as he re-entered the computer lab, attributing what he had seen to an over-active imagination caused by lack of sleep. *It's my own fault for staying up so late,* he thought. Nonetheless, he went right back to his research, immersing himself in all the replies he had received to his query about demons.

He had been at it for another half-hour or so when the silence was shattered yet again. This time he was briefly petrified by both the volume of the sound and the quickness with which it began and ended. As soon as the shock wore off, though, he was more concerned by the nature of the sound, which, given the circumstances, he should not have heard.

But there was no mistaking it. Right there in the computer lab, after midnight in a darkened and presumably deserted university building, the distinctive noise had filled the room. It was brief, but more than long enough to be recognized with certainty: the high-pitched crying of a baby.

Yusuf could scarcely believe what his ears had just heard because the presence of a baby, in that place at that hour, was almost impossible to imagine. But then he heard it again, as if it were trying to convince him that he was wrong. He jumped out of the chair like he had been stung, immediately feeling a chill come over him.

Now he was sure that something very abnormal was taking place in the building. He whispered a brief prayer, quickly but reluctantly signed out of the Friends List, and powered down the terminal. Then he got up and proceeded to leave the lab, still trying to come up with a theory as to how and why he had heard a baby crying in a university building in the middle of the night.

Walking down a corridor heading for the unlocked door through which he had entered, Yusuf kept thinking the same thought. This night couldn't possibly get any weirder. When it did, he thought his head would explode: every wall in the building seemed to echo with the sound of a little baby again, only this time it was laughing!

The laughter ended just as quickly as the crying had, but Yusuf's nerves were frayed, and he started to panic. He broke into a run, wanting nothing but to escape the madness of the place as quickly as possible. He kept running until he saw the door on his left, the one that was always left open for late-night access, so he slowed up and ... Locked!

"No, how is this possible?" he asked as he pressed again – harder this time – on the horizontal metal bar, but to no avail.

His fears were really getting the better of him now, so he started pounding on the door's thick safety glass, his voice whiny as he pleaded, "Open the door! Is anybody here?"

He got no answer other than a blend of his own echo with what were now the alternating laughs and cries of the baby. He covered his ears with his hands and shut his eyes tightly, crying, "Enough! Stop, you demon child!"

Silence returned as soon as he said that, so Yusuf had the chance to calm himself down a little, breathing in and out as slowly as he could manage. He had just about got the panting under control when he heard more noises: metal on metal, followed by the heavy footfalls of hard-soled shoes on

ROOM NUMBER 8

the marble floor. Not far away – and getting closer.

Each step he heard turned his anxiety up a notch until it met the definition of terror. They got closer and closer, just around the corner, and then a figure emerged from a side corridor, paused, and started coming towards him. Overwhelmed by fear, too scared even to run, Yousef retreated a few inches until his back was hard-up against the locked door, and there he awaited his fate.

Chapter 56

The security guard was bored as he carried out his routine inspection patrol through that part of campus. So when he approached the FIT building, he was actually grateful to hear the metallic clanging that usually signified some student's futile attempts to leave via the wrong door. Now he had to find the kid, show him the right way out, maybe have a laugh or two at his expense – all of which would be welcome breaks from the monotony of his job.

"Here is another terrified boy who has lost his way," the guard said to himself as he neared the door that was always left open, "just as surely as it says 'Mohammed' on my nametag." Then he laughed at his own little joke. Once he was inside, he walked down the corridor to its intersection with the one perpendicular, turned his head to the left, and saw Yusuf at the far end, leaning against the locked door.

The dim lighting prevented Mohammed from seeing much detail until he got close, and although he had got used to the looks of terror in the students' eyes, this time he was a little disturbed when he saw what the kid was doing. Even from two or three metres way, he could tell that Yusuf was breathing like a freight train, scratching the lower part of his chin hysterically, and his eyes focused exclusively on the guard's feet. That last part made the latter lower his own gaze, too, asking,

"Why are you staring at my shoes like that?"

ROOM NUMBER 8

He did not get an answer, and when he looked up again, he was totally taken aback: Yusuf was now standing right in front of him, almost nose to nose, and his expression showed not the slightest hint of fear. Quite the contrary, the kid's features radiated vigour and confidence.

Mohammed stepped back and asked nervously, "What's this? How did you get in my face so fast? What's going on?"

Then the guard felt his blood run cold as he heard a vicious female voice, much like the hiss of a snake, come out of Yusuf's mouth:

"You would understand nothing, human. Get away from me."

Mohammed had never encountered this kind of behaviour from a student before, and the voice was even stranger. He kept retreating, trying to buy time as he struggled to take stock of the situation, but soon his hand moved instinctively to the holster on his right hip.

He pulled out his handgun, brandishing it in front of the kid him like an unspoken warning, and shouted: "Are you trying to make fun of me? What's with the silly voice?" Yusuf continued to come forward, his cold glare fixed on the eyes of the guard, who kept retreating. This infuriated the latter, who suddenly decided to stand his ground and pointed the weapon at Yusuf's chest, hoping to deter any further advance. Mohammed got a very different result than he expected.

Chapter 57

It was very late when Yusuf got back from the FIT building. He felt a little dizzy as he approached the housing block, and parked his car in the first available space he could find inside the lot.

Walking back to his room, he was still trying to recall certain details of the past few hours. In particular, there was a gap in his memory that started when he had backed into the locked door and saw someone coming towards him, who turned out to be a security guard. The gap ended when a spectral black figure had crashed into the guard, leaving him moaning in pain on the floor and giving Yusuf the chance to leave the building.

The contrast between the two moments was not limited to the outward appearance of a reversal of fortunes. Instead, the transformation held a strong emotional component, in which feelings of fear and helplessness had been replaced by power and dominance. Once he entered the entrance of the housing block, he leaned against the wall and released a long sigh, trying to relieve the stress and confusion of not knowing exactly what had happened. Then he was frozen in place by the sound of Habiba's voice inside his head:

"He tried to hurt you. I did not allow that to happen."

Yusuf looked around to make sure there were no other students within earshot. Then he whispered, "Thank you, Habiba, but what happened to me there?"

"You asked for my help, and I gave you some of my power and firmness."

"I asked for it? How?"

"You were very frightened and you repeated the calling move."

He thought of her words a little before he nodded his head in understanding, then he remembered the more important thing, so he murmured, "But, why can't I remember the details of the transformation phase from fear to strength?"

Silence answered him.

He waited for a little while, then asked again:

"Habiba, why can't I remember it?"

"There must be a price for your protection my dear ... Now, come, go back to the room."

The softness with which she had pronounced that sentence had melted away his determination to understand the facts of what happened and pushed him to obey her by walking down the corridor until he reached Room Number 8. Then he stopped, briefly immobilized by the unusual sight before him.

His eyes narrowed as he realized that the door was ajar.

Yusuf looked at his wrist watch, which indicated one in the morning, and thought maybe Yaser had gone to the toilet, so he pushed the door open and stepped up and into the room. For the third time in the past few minutes, he froze up, instantly gripped by stress and suspicion by the sight of his friend, laying in his own bed.

He did not understand how Yaser could have gone to sleep with the door left open like that. But is he really asleep?

Yusuf ran his eyes around the room as he slowly walked further inside.

Chapter 58

When Yusuf woke up the next morning, he found Yaser standing before the long mirror in the corner of the room, examining his reflection in an unusual way. He pulled himself up into a seated position and said in a husky voice, "Good morning Yaser. Why are you staring at your face like that?"

It seemed like his friend had not heard the question. Yusuf kept looking at him for a whole minute, after which Yaser sighed. Then – without taking his eyes off his reflection – he answered:

"My eyes."

"Your eyes? Is something wrong with them?"

Yaser turned around and came near him, and Yusuf was astonished when he saw his best friend's eyes, the whites of which were completely red.

"Oh! What's that? What happened to them?"

Yaser answered with a shrug of his shoulders and an expression of that indicated he had no idea, then turned back towards the mirror, saying, "I should have the doctor at the campus clinic take a look as soon as possible."

Yusuf agreed, then he remembered something.

"Yaser, why did you leave the door ajar when you went to bed last night?"

His friend was putting on some outdoor clothes as he answered, "I didn't do it on purpose, of course, but I don't remember how or when I fell asleep last night."

"I know it can happen," Yusuf said, "but I'm not used to this kind of thing from you. Forgetting the door like that can bring very bad consequences."

"There's a first time for everything, right?"

"Yes," Yusuf muttered as he headed out the door towards the toilets and showers.

Once he was gone, Yaser finished getting dressed, grabbed his books, and went to his car. As he walked to the parking lot, he wondered why he had felt reticent to be up-front Yusuf about what had happened the previous night whilst his friend was out – and about a weird point regarding his eyes. Although they were really red, he felt no pain at all.

Chapter 59

As he returned to the room, Yusuf started thinking again about what had happened at the FIT building: the legless man, the baby crying and then laughing, and then the incident with the guard.

He understood why Habiba had attacked the latter, and therefore the euphoric senses of power and satisfaction that had filled his heart at that moment, exactly like he felt after she got back at Mr. John for him. However, he could think of no explanation for that man with no legs or the presence of an infant inside the building.

Then something very worrisome occurred to him: the security guard. Yusuf started wondering how badly he had been hurt, whether it was just a few bruises, or maybe the man had sustained serious injuries. Either way, he also worried that the guard might report what had happened; they could be looking for him already, determined to punish him.

He was very close to the room when the fixed telephone for that end of the hall rang. He stopped before his door; he had to choose quickly between ignoring it or going back to the wall near the entrance to the toilets section, where the telephone was hung.

He made his decision quickly and hurried through the corridor until he reached the phone and picked it up.

"Hello?" he said.

He heard a feminine voice, a little hoarse, saying, "Hello, good morning."

"Good morning. Which room do you want?"

That was the typical question callers were asked. Then whoever had answered would alert the guys in that room that there was someone on the phone for them. This time, however, Yusuf was stunned when the caller gave him an entirely unexpected answer:

"I want you."

"Excuse me?! What did you say?"

The woman laughed, softly and femininely, and said, "Obviously I'm the first girl to call you. Is that right?"

Yusuf rubbed his eyes with his free hand, then used it to smoothen his hair before answering nervously, "I just woke up; it seems that my mind is not yet ready to understand what's happening right now."

"Do you really not know about random matchmaking communications, specifically random dating calls?"

He tried to ease his stress with humour, replying, "I know telecommunications, yes, the microwave, and the wireless, but the matchmaking communications, no. I haven't studied that in any of my university courses yet."

He heard the woman laugh again, then her hoarse voice said, "I like your light spirit. What's your name?"

Yusuf's eyes widened a little and he smiled in surprise and disbelief. Having grown up in a very conservative society, he had very little experience with members of the opposite sex – which was to say none.

"Oh my God! A girl wants to get to know me. This is really happening!"

"For sure it is happening. Now tell me: what is your name?"

"Yusuf, from Room Number 8."

"Hi Yusuf. I am Noha."

"Hello Noha, a beautiful name for a beautiful girl, for sure."

She sounded happy as she asked, "How can you be sure?"

"She who warbles with her voice, whose laugh pleases the air, and whose name inspires the mind, cannot hold but a charming face," he replied.

"Oh, what's with all the flirting? Where did you hear that?"

It was Yusuf's turn to laugh.

"My mind, which has just woken up is the one that crafted those words after hearing you."

"Okay, you with the awakened mind. When do your lectures start today?"

"My lectures? Oh no! I've completely forgotten everything! I'm going to my class if I don't move leave immediately. My apologies Noha."

She laughed, then added: "I am the one who owes you an apology since my call distracted you from preparing for your lectures. Come on, go now."

"Will you call another time?"

"Maybe. Goodbye, Yusuf."

Chapter 60

Whilst Yusuf was at the preparatory year building later that day, several different feelings inside him became conflated in an unusual way. All at once, he felt bewilderment over the strange incidents at the IT building, high anxiety over the possibility that he might be summoned by university officials because of what happened to the guard, and a rush of happiness because he had decided to answer the telephone a few hours ago and therefore had his first experience of random dating calls.

During one of the breaks between lectures, Yusuf was sitting with his best friend to have hot drinks and doughnuts like they used to do and suddenly asked, "Tell me Yaser, have you ever heard of random dating calls?"

Yaser paused for several moments before he answered.

"I may have overheard some guys talking about that concept a while back, but I didn't pay any attention to them."

"Apparently they're calls from girls in the cities near the universities who want to have fun and get to know each other ... and perhaps for other, bigger purposes."

"And who told you that definition?"

"No one did. I've lived the experience myself."

Yaser contorted his face into a mask of mock shock and outrage, bringing the usual smile from Yusuf.

Then the former asked: "You've lived the experience? What do you mean?"

"This morning I answered the telephone near the toilets and the caller was one of these girls ... Her name is Noha."

Yaser was sipping his coffee when he heard this, and although he tried to control himself, he failed, spitting some of the dark brown liquid onto the table. Yusuf pulled back in his seat a little, then said laughingly,

"Man, what's wrong? Pull yourself together."

Yaser coughed several times, his face turning red and Yusuf watching him sympathetically. Finally he caught his breath and said in a hoarse voice,

"Who is this Noha? Give me more details."

Yusuf told him about the discussion they had. "Wow. So my best friend is getting to know a female stranger ... Who would've imagined that?"

Then he scratched his head, thinking for a few seconds before he added:

"But do such communications not hold risks?"

Yusuf frowned.

"Which kind of risks do you mean?"

"I'm not sure, but for example, maybe the telephone lines here are bugged?"

"I don't think so. From my brief discussion with some of the other students, I found that some of them have been talking to these random dating girls for quite a while without anyone bothering them about it."

"Okay," Yaser allowed, "but what are you expecting from such conversations?"

Yusuf shrugged and took a bite of his doughnut before he replied.

"It only started this morning, so I haven't made up my mind about that yet," he said. "In any event, I don't have any way of contacting her, and I don't know if she'll ever call me again, but I'll keep my hopes up."

Yaser laughed.

"So now you'll be exhausted from running to the phone every time it rings," he said with a wink and a smile. "You're so lucky, my friend, your efforts in answering the phone from time to time have finally paid off!"

Yusuf smiled broadly, replying, "I had no idea about this random calling or random dating. My efforts to answer the phone have always been for purely humanitarian reasons!"

Chapter 61

When they were both back at the room that afternoon, Yaser lay on his bed to put in the eye drops prescribed by the doctor at the university clinic.

Yusuf noticed and said, "I'm sorry. I meant to ask you about the redness in your eyes and totally forgot. What did the doctor say?"

After administering the drops, Yaser sat up and lightly dabbed the wetness from around his eyes with tissue paper. Then he got up somewhat excitedly and started to change his clothes.

"Your mind is preoccupied with the anonymous girl, my friend," he quipped. "As for the doctor, he didn't find anything specific, just told me to use these drops regularly, and hopefully my eyes will go back to normal."

"I hope that's soon, man," Yusuf told him "Actually, the redness seems to have eased a lot already."

"Thank God."

A few minutes later, they were both outside, heading towards the green area in the middle of the housing block, where a friendly football match had been scheduled. They arrived there to find Ashraf and most of the other students from their hall warming up.

Shortly thereafter, they divided themselves into two teams and got started. Things began calmly, but the tempo steadily increased, and the match grew more and more competitive, with neither side wanting to lose.

Yusuf literally felt the intensity as he dribbled the ball towards the opposing team's goal and a student named Omar attempted a slide tackle. Yusuf got the ball beyond past him, then tried to jump out of the way, but not in time: Omar's tackle found the side of his left ankle.

Yusuf cried out in pain as he fell to the ground. He lay there grimacing as he clutched at his ankle, and play was soon stopped. Several students came over to check on him, and Yaser arrived first, getting down on his knees to examine his friend's injury.

"I think it's just a bruise," he said, "nothing serious, thank God."

Soon Yusuf made it to a sitting position, and as Yaser started to help him stand, he was joined by Omar, who also extended his hand and said jokingly, "Come on, Captain ... Don't be dramatic." Yusuf grabbed his hand, too, and the guys pulled him to his feet.

After Yusuf took a few steps to test the ankle, he concluded that Yaser had been right: the injury was not a bad one. He also realized, however, that he would no longer be much help on the pitch, so he declared himself done for the day and limped back to his room for a rest.

Chapter 62

Over the next couple of days, Yusuf's sore ankle forced him to abandon his habit of running to the phone whenever he heard it ringing. Others had stepped in to pick up the slack, especially Yaser.

Yusuf was alone in the room now, smiling as he recalled how, that first evening following his injury, the phone rang and he exerted himself to get up from his bed, then started moving slowly towards the door. But Yaser had stopped him and offered to go find out who the caller was and who they wanted to talk to. Yusuf had made a great show of that, shouting,

"I can't believe what's happening! Yaser, by himself, rushing to answer the phone? It's the first time ... History will record it ... But is it for the sake of my comfort? Or are you trying to take Noha from me?"

Yaser had laughed heartily at that. Then, as he opened the door, he asked, "Would you deny me if that were my real goal?"

Yusuf replied without hesitation:

"You are the friend of my life, the only one for whom I wish exactly what I wish for myself."

Yaser had smiled and commented, "I expected no other answer, my friend. Thank you."

Although the call was not from Noha, Yaser had not grumbled when he returned to the room. Rather, he had been happy that he could comfort his friend.

At this, moment, however, Yaser was not there, so when

the phone started ringing, someone else had to answer. Yusuf noticed that the ringing had not lasted long, which meant that someone from one of the rooms closest to the telephone had probably picked up. Less than a minute later, he heard footsteps approaching, followed by knocking on his door.

He got up from his chair and opened the door to find Zuhair there.

"Hello, Yusuf," he said. "The call is for you this time."

Yusuf nodded to him and gave him a quick look of appreciation. "Thank you, Zuhair."

"How's your foot? Is it getting better?"

Yusuf put on his shoes, stepped into the corridor, and closed the door behind him, saying, "Thank God, all that's left is some very slight pain when I walk." Zuhair patted his shoulder supportively as he walked beside him along the corridor. "Get well soon, man," he said as they neared the telephone and parted ways. "We want you to make a quick return to the pitch."

When he reached the phone, Yusuf put it to his ear and said with both eagerness and anxiety, "Hello, who is calling?"

He was hoping to hear Noha's voice, but at the same time, he was afraid that the call was from a university official. He was relieved when he heard the feminine voice say,

"Hello, Yusuf. Did you miss me?"

He whispered, "Oh, Noha ... You have a beautiful voice. How could not I miss it?"

Predictably, she expressed appreciation for the compliment, but what she said next came as an unimaginable shock.

Chapter 63

"Are you positive you hadn't told her about it before?" That was Yaser's reaction after he had returned to the room and Yusuf started explaining what Noha had said to him during her call.

"A hundred percent sure! That was the first time I spoke to her since I got hurt. And as soon as I got on the phone with her, she asked about my leg. How could she have known?!"

"You must have asked her the same question. What did she say?"

"Of course I did," Yusuf said, "but her answer was even more confusing."

"How? What did she say?"

Yusuf nervously scratched at the area under his chin and replied, "She said she could know anything about me whenever she wants!"

Once again, Yaser went into his exaggerated surprise routine, his eyes and mouth opened as far as they would go. Unusually, however, this time Yusuf was not amused by his friend's display.

Yaser pressed the issue, saying, "So we're supposed to believe that this Noha is the female Arab version of James Bond? A super-spy who know everything? Come on, man! Tell me something I can believe. She's trying to get your attention, nothing more."

But Yusuf was sure there was more to it than that. He

looked his friend straight in the eye and asked,

"If that's the case, then how did she know I got hurt?"

Yaser did not answer right away, wondering if he had made up his mind too quickly. He thought about it for several moments, but then concluded that his first impression was the right one: there had to be a logical explanation.

"Someone else must have told her," he insisted. "There's no other way for the news to have reached her. Maybe this female James Bond has placed a secret agent right here in our midst!"

Yaser had made his point with yet another little joke, but Yusuf took the idea very seriously. He wondered if the girl might also have some kind of relationship with another guy in their hall, and if she did, who might it be?

Chapter 64

The following afternoon, as he returned to the dorm from the preparatory year building, Yusuf noticed that several students were gathered in the corridor. Even from a distance, he could hear the stress in their voices. At first he could hear only scattered phrases, but as he got closer, he grew increasingly concerned:

"There is no power and no strength except with Allah."

"Sad, but it happens."

"Oh, the poor guy."

"Where is he now?"

"The university clinic,"

"How did it happen?"

"No one's sure yet."

"Has his roommate been informed?"

The last question was asked just as Yusuf reached the group, and it bothered him greatly that there was no sign of Yaser. He wanted to ask about his friend directly, but he dreaded the answer, so all he could manage was a generic greeting.

"Hey guys, how's it going?"

Everyone turned to greet him with the same anxious faces, and Ashraf said, "Hi Yusuf. Have you heard what had happened a little while ago?"

Yusuf's heart skipped a beat, a sense of foreboding welling up inside him and coming out as questions: "A little while ago? No, what happened? Does it have anything to do with Yaser?"

"No, not Yaser ... It's Omar."

Yusuf was relieved to learn that his best friend was okay, but the concern and stress were still written on his face.

"Omar? What's wrong with him?"

Now it was Mansour, the head of their housing block, who spoke up.

"This is exactly why we need to go so see him at the clinic," he told the others. "People are spreading rumours, and we have no idea how much of what they're saying is true."

"But what have you heard about it so far?" Yusuf asked.

Again, it was Mansour who answered: "A serious injury to his foot. Apparently he was on the stairs, coming down the hill, and somehow lost his balance and took a bad fall. That's why we're going to see him, so he can tell us what happened."

"We're going now, Yusuf," Ashraf said when Mansour had finished. "You want to join us?"

"Sure, just give me a minute to put my books in the room."

Chapter 65

"Good night," Yusuf said that night as he switched off the main overhead lights, the small night lamp keeping the room a step or two from complete darkness.

"Good night," Yaser answered, an accompanying yawn signalling that he would not be awake much longer. Sure enough, within minutes of closing his eyes, he was fast asleep.

Meanwhile, Yusuf was stretched out on his bed, still awake and feeling a bit sad as he recalled the conversation he had had with Yaser about Omar's mishap. The poor guy had returned to his room in the residential compound on crutches, and the doctor said his left leg would stay in a plaster cast for at least a month!

Eventually Yusuf fell asleep, too, and shortly thereafter, something compelled his hand to move up towards his neck. There his fingers started touching that spot under his chin ever so softly, and soon the tickling sensation made his skin feel itchy. That's when he woke up, exactly like the previous time.

As he soon as he opened his eyes, he was immediately aware of Habiba's presence, because his body felt cold and stiff and did not respond to commands from his brain. He was lying on his side facing the wall, so although he could feel her behind him, he could not see how she manifested her presence. He closed his eyes and whispered,

"Hello, Habiba! I missed you."

He felt her moving behind him as she whispered back, "I

spent most of my day inside you."

The delicious numbness enveloped his feet first, then started moving slowly up his legs. Habiba asked him lovingly,

"Did you like what I did for you?"

At first, he could not connect what she said with the incidents of the past few days, but he soon came up with what felt like a strong possibility.

"You mean Omar?"

"Of course!" she said. "Who else caused you pain? Didn't you notice that his injury is to the same foot that kicked you?"

Once again, Yusuf was happy that she had wanted to avenge him, but the feeling was tempered by sorrow at what happened to his hall-mate.

"Thank you for all that you've been doing, Habiba, but Omar didn't intend to hurt me! We were just playing!"

His ears hurt from the echo of her devilish giggle.

"How weak your interactions are as human beings. You allow yourselves to get hurt without taking revenge, but let me remind you of an important thing."

"What's that?"

"You are no longer the sole owner of your body! I now share this ownership," Habiba told him. "Whoever or whatever hurts you also hurts me, so what causes you distress and pain will taste my revenge and retribution. Do you understand?"

The amazing numbness reached the mid-way point in his body at that moment, so he lost his focus on the conversation and did not reply to her question. He sank into an exquisite sea of excitement that he had never experienced except with her presence inside him ... and controlling his body!

Chapter 66

In the following days, Yusuf was tormented by an internal struggle between his heart and his mind. He was living a real moral crisis. On the one hand, he very much enjoyed both the pleasure Habiba gave him and the power he felt when she acted on his behalf. On the other, however, his conscience reproached him for dealing with a demon, particularly one who interfered with other people, even hurting them without mercy.

He thought back to the lab supervisor's car crash, the attack on the security guard, the manipulation that caused Yaser to smash his own stereo, and – especially – the severe injury that Omar had suffered to his foot. Over the past few days, he had been tortured by guilt every time he saw his hall-mate, knowing that he had played a role in the guy's suffering.

This was no longer confined to his own personal issues. At least four people had been directly affected in some way by the agreement he had concluded with the demon. The more he thought about it, the more difficult questions he had to ask himself. *Is this what I wanted? Do I really want to be a human time bomb that can go off in the face of whoever gets near it? Do I want this to go on?*

Deep inside, he had to acknowledge basic things. The first was that no, he did not like the feeling of being a bomb. The second was his vulnerability towards Habiba and the pleasure he felt whenever she was inside him. He had no

idea how to reconcile these conflicted feelings. Then he remembered something else he had to admit:
Noha!
There had been numerous calls in the past few days, including some prolonged conversations in which they had dived deep into their respective personalities and developed intimate feelings for one another. He was getting attached to her, but he had not told her anything about Habiba. Nor had he decided whether he would tell her in the future or keep his secret to himself.

Chapter 67

"Oh my God, so the British intelligence lady has finally revealed the secret?" Yaser said merrily the next evening.

Yusuf smiled and nodded his head in confirmation, saying, "Yes, that's what happened in our call today."

"What are you waiting for, man? Tell me what happened."

"She told me that she's part of a group of friends, each one of whom is in a random dating relationship with a student at the university. And every day, they all share information with each, stuff they've heard whilst talking with their guys."

"Oh my God! In other words, this is a comprehensive network of intelligence agents and there are male spies among us, all of them in relationships with these women!"

That got them both laughing uncontrollably, tears rolling down their cheeks. It took a couple of minutes for them to calm down and wipe away the tears. It was Yusuf who first regained the ability to speak intelligibly: "This is so weird! I never imagined that such a thing could happen, but this is the reality."

Then Yaser added, "This means there's probably another guy here in the hall who's in a relationship with one of these girls. Who could it be?"

Yusuf shrugged his shoulders. "Not necessarily. It could be someone from another hall who knows someone from ours. It's not an easy thing to figure out."

"Anyway," Yaser declared with a wink and a smile, "from

now on, I will watch my tongue and make sure I stay decent in everything I say and do so that one of the local female British intelligence agents falls in love with me and wants to communicate with my modest character."

"I wish you all the best in your endeavours, my friend," Yusuf answered with a laugh. "As for me, I was destined to answer the telephone that morning and initiate a relationship with Agent 008."

"Eight?! There is it again – long live my favourite number!" Yaser exclaimed. "But wait a minute. Was she the one who gave you her secret code number?"

"No, I selected that number for her, but she gave me another number."

"What do you mean?"

Yusuf smiled knowingly.

"The number of the landline telephone in her room," he said. "She gave me her home address, too – to feel her presence."

Chapter 68

The following evening, Yusuf and Yaser ate dinner at a fast-food restaurant in one of the city's shopping malls, then drove back to campus. Walking from the parking area to the residential compound, they chatted about the most important thing on the minds of all students at that time: the final exams for the second semester.

Reaching their block and walking down the corridor to their room, they were still discussing the exams as they reached their door. Yusuf inserted his key in the lock and turned it. As soon as he heard the bolt slide over, he gave the door a little push and ...

The door moved only a few centimetres before it stopped.

Yusuf's eyes narrowed a bit. He pushed the door a little harder, then harder still, but it only moved another centimetre or so. It felt like something very heavy was on the other side, keeping the door from opening.

Yusuf felt a sudden itch on the skin under his chin, so he raised his free hand to scratch at it as Yaser asked,

"What's the problem, mate?"

Yusuf retreated a bit, still scratching away, and muttered distractedly,

"The room. It refuses to let us in."

"What are you saying, guy? Let me try."

Yaser put his shoulder against the door and felt a little movement as he leaned into it, but then it stopped again.

ROOM NUMBER 8

He tried again, pressing against the door with all his strength, but nothing happened, and silently he cursed the latest incidence of abnormality. Like everyone else, he was already stressed out over the impending exams, and ... *now this: like we need more to worry about.*

Just then, they both heard the sound of footsteps in the corridor and turned to see who it was. Yaser shouted, "Hey, Ashraf, can you give us a hand?"

Ashraf waved as he approached, then shook hands with them.

"Hey, neighbours! What kind of help do you need?"

Yusuf motioned vaguely at the door as Yaser said,

"The door won't open. There might be a problem with the hinges or something. I don't know what the problem is, but we both tried, and no matter how hard we pushed, it wouldn't move more than a few centimetres!"

"Let me have a look," Ashraf said. He could see how little the door had opened despite the guys' best efforts, but he wanted to see how it responded to pressure, so he reached out and put his hand on it.

Yusuf and Yaser were stunned by what happened as he did so.

Chapter 69

In a secret place away from prying eyes, the soldiers worked in a very organized way. They toiled tirelessly and relentlessly, but also efficiently, functioning as a single unit, as all of them had been trained to do since the day they had joined.

Today, however, there was something very different.

Without exception, all of them had received urgent orders from an unknown authority in an unusual way which they would never understand. And yet, without taking a single moment trying to comprehend the order, they all left the work they were doing, and the army moved as one unit to execute the order, driven by an invisible power that none of the soldiers could recognize.

En route to the target, they marched without respite along all available paths. They worked together to surmount high hills and other obstacles, ignoring those who fell dead because they had neither the will to stop, nor the ability to retreat.

Although they knew nothing about the destination, its location, or how far it was from their starting point, they knew they had reached it as soon they arrived. They all stopped on top of it for a few moments to organize their lines and let a few late arrivals catch up.

Then, although not a single one of them had a watch or any other way to tell time, the entire army moved out as one, advancing to attack the target:

Room Number 8.

Chapter 70

The door swung all the way open as soon as Ashraf's fingers touched it. He turned towards Yusuf and Yaser and had to laugh at the looks of utter astonishment on their faces. He stepped aside, motioned for them to enter, and teased,

"Glad to be of service, gentlemen. Please come ..."

Ashraf stopped mid-sentence because he saw their facial expressions change instantly from amazement to horror. Yusuf took a step backward, scratching vigorously at the skin under his chin. Ashraf turned quickly to look into the room again, and what he saw filled him with dread, disgust, and denial.

"No God but God!" he shouted. "What is this?!"

Inside the room, all three of them could see a black rain falling on the floor!

But it was not rain. Rather, it was an army of huge black ants flooding in through the gaps around the overhead fluorescents.

None of the three students could understand what they were seeing, but they knew they had to act quickly. The ants were falling in unimaginable numbers, and as soon they hit the floor, they spread out across their target area: if they were not stopped, they would soon overrun every piece of furniture, every countertop, every nook and cranny in the room, making it impossible to root them out.

Ashraf was the first to recover his senses. He picked up a shoe next to the doorway, took a few steps inside, and got to work, squashing some underfoot while using the shoe in his hand to dispatch those on the walls and furniture. Yaser quickly followed his lead, and soon the two of them were slaughtering the invaders as fast as they could.

But not Yusuf. He remained in the corridor, watching in silence as his friends dealt with the problem.

After they had been at it for a few minutes, Yaser shouted, "This won't work! They're coming in faster than we can kill them!"

Then he felt a sting on his arm. "Ouch," he cried as he swatted the ant off of him. "I hate insects even more now!"

Then he turned to Ashraf and shouted, "Look out! There's one on your right shoulder!"

"Gross!" Ashraf said as he cast it off with his free hand. "I think you're right. There are too many of them."

He looked around the room for a few seconds, then yelled: "I have a better idea!""

Ashraf rushed to the corner, picked up his secret weapon, carried it back to the middle of the room, and hit the switch. The vacuum cleaner roared to life, and Yaser felt relieved.

"That's a much better idea!" he told his hall-mate. "Show no mercy. Get every one of them."

Ashraf needed no encouragement. He ran the nozzle through the ranks of the ants, sucking them up with ease. After a few moments, the influx of ants falling from the ceiling decreased, then stopped completely.

"Fantastic!" Yaser said. "But we still need to check the furniture and the wardrobe and shake the sheets and blankets."

Ashraf nodded in agreement, and together they hunted down the stragglers until all resistance ended. The battle won, they both wanted only to rest, so they each grabbed a chair and sat down.

Chapter 71

Yusuf was still in the doorway. As Ashraf and Yaser had dashed into the room to fight the ant army, Yusuf had heard the voice of Habiba, strong and stern, inside his mind: "Do not enter the room. Stay right here."

He obeyed her, but whispered, "As you wish, Habiba. But why?"

There was a tone of suppressed anger in her curt answer: "A doomed room. Don't go inside now. Wait!"

Thus it was that Yusuf stayed outside the room, following what was happening in silence until his friends had got rid of all the ants. Only then did he walk inside, keeping a watchful eye out for any remnants of the enemy.

"Thank you for repelling the invasion," he said. "You're welcome," Ashraf replied, "but I'm curious. We've had a scorpion, a rat, and now ants. What will it be next time?"

The attempt at humour drew no response from the others. Yusuf went and sat on his bed with his back to the wall, whilst Yaser started scratching different parts of his body, complaining, "I hate ants, especially those giant ones: they look like dinosaurs. Seeing just one of them makes me freak out, let alone a whole army!"

With that, Ashraf stood up and headed for the door, saying, "God help you, guys. Time for me to go. Good night."

Yaser walked him out, shaking his hand and expressing appreciation for his assistance. "Thank you, Ashraf," he said.

You're our best neighbour!"

Ashraf smiled back at him and patted his shoulder as he left.

Yaser stopped to have a look at the door, paying close attention to its hinges as he opened and closed it a few times. Then he walked back to his part of the room and started changing his clothes. His voice carried a reproachful tone when he spoke to his friend:

"What's wrong with you, Yusuf? Once again, we had a real problem, and you just stood there, watching me and Ashraf take care of it and not doing anything to help us!"

It seemed to him that Yusuf was not listening, so he was about to repeat himself, but then his friend asked:

"Is that really our biggest concern now? Me watching without helping?"

Yaser realized at once what he meant, and deep inside, he had to agree. It was indeed annoying that Yusuf had not stepped up, but the real problem was that they had just gone through yet another inexplicable experience. In fact, it occurred to him, the really weird part wasn't even the invasion of ants. *It was the door: how was it possible that it was immovably heavy for me and Yusuf, then completely normal as soon Ashraf touched it?*

Frustration mixed with distress as Yaser scanned the place with his eyes and shouted,

"What do you want from us, room?! Speak up!"

Chapter 72

Both Yaser and Yusuf woke up feeling exhausted the following morning. As had had happened after the episodes with the scorpion and the rat, their sleep had been too little and too disturbed to have been of much value. Fatigue and misery were etched into their faces as they trudged towards the toilets section.

As they walked down the corridor, Yusuf was once again tortured by remorse when he saw Omar moving gingerly on his crutches. He wished he could confess everything and ask for forgiveness, just to get rid of that feeling of guilt, but he did nothing of the sort. He just greeted him, asked about his health, and wished him a quick recovery.

When they finished washing up, Yusuf and Yaser returned to their room, got dressed, and started gathering what they needed for their class work that day. When the sound of the telephone rang out, they both stiffened, exchanging looks full of both indecision and expectation.

"Could it be her?" Yusuf asked.

"It's hard to say if you don't have an agreement about the exact timing, but it's possible. Why not?"

"Possible is good enough for me." Yusuf headed out the door and down the corridor towards the telephone.

It was Noha.

Chapter 73

As soon as Yaser woke up, he realized it was the last day of the semester before final exams. He slowly pulled himself upright in his bed and looked across at Yusuf's. He blinked his eyes a few times to make sure he was seeing straight, but there was no mistake: it was empty.

He rubbed the sleep out his eyes, took a deep breath, and muttered,

"I've got to get used to Yusuf's weird surprises. God help him to overcome whatever he's going through."

He grabbed some soap and a towel and dragged himself down the corridor towards the showers, expecting to see Yusuf on the telephone, but he was not there. He kept going, got himself washed up, and headed back to the room.

When he got there, he got dressed and started rounding up the books and other materials he need for his classes. He was almost done when he heard a strange sound. It was very close and sounded like a rattle of some sort, but it stopped before he could either identify what he had heard or determine where it came from. Still on edge from all the madness he had seen in the room, Yaser could feel his body trembling, but he tried to stay calm as he looked around for the source of the sound. Then he heard something again, but this time it was a different sound. In fact, it was several: rubbing, scratching, and a couple of thuds.

And now he sure: all of it was coming from inside the wardrobe.

Unbidden, several questions popped into Yaser's mind. *What is it now? Another rat? Something else?* Whatever it was, he worried that the door might fall off its hinges like the last time. *And if anything, this time it sounds bigger!* That meant he had to move quickly.

He looked around the room for something he could use as a weapon. Eyeing the vacuum cleaner, he noticed the long metal pipe between the handle and the nozzle. After disconnecting the pipe at both ends, he made sure he had a good grip and approached the wardrobe.

"Thank you, room, for this wonderful morning!" he muttered, trying to distract himself from his own fears.

It did little good, and his hands were shaking as he used one of them to hold the pipe high in the air, ready to strike, and the other to grasp the door handle. He inhaled a deep breath and whispered, "God, grant me strength."

He whipped the door open as hard as he could, stepping back to let it swing clear and expose whatever was inside. What he saw there was worse than any of the thoughts he had had earlier.

Oh, no!

Chapter 74

Yaser had considered numerous possibilities before he flung the wardrobe door open, but this one had not occurred to him, and none of the others could have caused him so much concern. Although he no longer felt exposed to immediate physical danger, what he saw was profoundly disturbing because it reaffirmed his worst fears – and no mere metal pipe could do anything about it.

For on the floor of the wardrobe, knees drawn up to his chest, surprised and obviously confused, lay his best friend.

"Yusuf? What are you doing in there?" was all Yaser could say.

Yusuf did not respond at first. He remained in what was basically the foetal position, looking like he was more asleep than awake. More worrisomely from Yaser's perspective, he was also completely naked! Yusuf finally exhibited some sign of awareness, however limited, as he grabbed a shirt from one of the shelves inside the wardrobe and tried to cover himself. Then, his voice unsteady and laden with disarray, he said,

"Where ... am I?"

Out of patience with his friend's bizarre behaviour, Yaser spoke angrily.

"Are you asking where you are? Man, you're in the last place – and the last condition – anyone should be found! Here you are, curled in a ball sleeping in a dark corner of a wardrobe! What's wrong with you?! Last time, you were hiding under your bed, and today I found you in the wardrobe. God knows where you'll be next time. You might wake up and find yourself in the showers or the toilet!"

"Believe me, Yaser, I don't know how I ended up here. I was sleeping in my bed."

"That's the problem," Yaser snapped. "You don't know what happened, or what will happen next. There's something wrong, and I asked you right from the beginning to open your heart and let me help me you, but you refused and you were arrogant and now here you are, living with the ridiculous consequences."

Yusuf could find no words with which to answer. His mind was muddled and he could not think clearly. He felt cold and ashamed, and was still flush with surprise at what had just happened. His only visible response to his friend's outburst was to scratch compulsively under his chin.

Yaser sighed a couple of times to calm himself down, then said, "Anyway, I've got classes to attend, so I'm going now. It's too late to get into now, but this evening I expect to have a long conversation with you so you can come clean about all the details of what's happening to you."

He stopped for a moment, pointed to his own chin, and added, "Including that weird habit that's taken you over ever since we came to university!"

Chapter 75

Most of the day had passed, and it had been extraordinarily difficult for Yusuf. It had started very shamefully when his friend found him naked inside the wardrobe, followed by an inner conversation and argument about that specific point with Habiba. And then for the rest of the day, he had been badly distracted, losing his ability to focus during the crucial revision sessions on which he, like most students, relied in order in order to score well on the final exams.

And now here he was sitting on his bed, his back both literally and figuratively against the wall, as Yaser sat on a chair facing him. The scene was identical to the previous time, when Yusuf had refused to disclose any details, but after all that had taken place since then, this time he knew his friend would insist on getting some answers.

"My dear Yusuf," Yaser began, "I'm your best friend and I care about your wellbeing, so please tell me everything, and let me try to help you. Please. Don't let me down like you did last time."

Yaser could see the internal struggle playing itself out on Yusuf's face, so he felt pity for him, but he also reminded himself that retreating now and not uncovering the truth about what his friend was going through would lead to unpredictable – and possibly disastrous – results. He just hoped that Yusuf would finally understand this and start cooperating with him.

"Everything started on the ground floor of our house in Makkah during the last year of secondary school ... "

Yaser silently thanked God when Yusuf started narrating his story. He listened carefully, refraining from any interruption to avoid any kind of argument that might stop his friend from sharing the rest of the details. At the same time, he could not keep his facial expressions from revealing all or most of what he felt as Yusuf shared the secrets he had been keeping. Astonishment, anxiety, fear, and several other reactions swept over him as his friend spoke.

Eventually, Yusuf appeared to be summing up. "What happened yesterday might be sleepwalking ... I don't know, but for sure it's an undesirable development of my situation when I do things I don't remember. No one wants to go to sleep without knowing where or how he will wake up!"

Despite his continuing unease and how difficult it had been to confess his secrets, Yusuf felt relieved because now he had someone with whom he could share the burden he had been carrying.

"That's the whole story," he said at last. "Do you believe it?"

Yaser felt overwhelmed by all the secrets his friend had just disclosed. For several moments, he could do nothing but close his eyes and rub his temples, hoping it might help him digest the story he had just heard, connect its parts together, and see the full picture.

Although he had heard stories about demons or evil spirits – jinn, in local parlance – when he was a child, what was happening between Yusuf and Habiba was on a completely different level. In addition, hearing tales about people you don't know cannot be compared with the shock of being an indirect part of a real story.

If virtually anyone else told him what he had just heard, he would not have believed them, but his long and close association with Yusuf made him trust every single word. And he wanted to help. Yaser finally opened his eyes, ready to reply and discuss, but instead he recoiled like he'd been snake-bitten. He kept retreating, trying to maintain distance and keeping his eyes locked on what had scared him.

His oldest and dearest friend, Yusuf!

PART III
THE WAR WITHIN

Chapter 76

"You should not have known, wretched human!"

The content of the sentence did not scare Yaser nearly as much as the voice that came out from between Yusuf's lips when he pronounced it. It was a sharply feminine voice, but also similar to the hissing of a snake. The voice was harsh and menacing in a way that was so different from Yusuf's peaceful character.

By contrast, Yaser's voice was very weak because his throat was dry, and because he was trembling from the shock of what had just transpired. He whispered, "I seek refuge with God from the cursed Satan."

As he said that, he watched the features on Yusuf's face go back to something more familiar. The look of grim cruelty that had accompanied the creepy sentence disappeared, and when his friend spoke again, it was in his own voice.

"No, Habiba, my friend Yaser is a red line I would never let you cross!" Yusuf said, his tone defiant and resolute. "Do you hear me?"

Yaser was relieved when he heard Yusuf's words, especially since they were articulated in his own voice, but he kept his distance to be on the safe side. He felt pain as he tried to absorb what was happening. He retreated some more and pointed a finger at his friend, shouting,

"Yusuf, this is madness! This demon is an imminent danger threatening you, me, and all the people around you. You have to get rid of it by any means possible and as quickly as you can!"

Yusuf let out a short scream, and the twisted muscles in his face reflected the internal pain he was suffering. Then he jumped to his feet with unusual lightness and grace. He paused for a second, then started to move towards his friend, scratching his chin violently.

Yaser backed off again, waving an arm at him, crying, "Wait! Stop!"

Yusuf kept coming.

Yaser tried to retreat some more but lost his balance when the back of his leg struck his bed, causing him to collapse onto it.

"Yusuf! What are you doing? I'm your friend! Please, man! Don't get any closer to me, please!!"

Yusuf kept coming.

Although Yaser had never imagined any kind of physical confrontation with his best friend, here it was, about to happen. He had to protect himself, even if he had no desire to hurt his friend. His mind raced as he tried to think of a solution, but there was no time. Then suddenly, the contest was on. And what a contest it was!

Chapter 77

He suddenly made a mad dash for the door, slowing down to pull it open and sprinting down the corridor, then out of the dorm. Then he turned left, running as fast as he could and completely ignoring the surprised looks of the students who watched him go by. He had only one aim in mind: he had to put as much distance as he could, as quickly as he could, between himself and his best friend!

He had not though it possible, but he had got the best of the demon. Just when Habiba had been about to turn her supernatural strength on Yaser, he had regained control over his own body. *All thanks to God,* Yusuf thought now as he kept running as fast as he could. He had no idea how long it would be before she turned the tables on him, however, so he had to keep running. That way, if and when she took control again and tried to use his body as a weapon against his friend, there would be more distance between them.

As he ran, he reflected on how painful and frustrating it was to have become a danger to everyone around him, not only when he was asleep, but also when he was awake to see, hear, and feel the harm his body could do to others without his being able to stop it. He wiped the tears out of his eyes and pressed on, running and running and running some more, until he could no longer catch his breath and had a burning sensation in his chest that forced him to stop. He panted hard, turning around in circles as he tried to identify his location.

He had reached the far end of the residential compound area and could see the highway that ran next to the university. Now he felt indecision over what to do next. The sounds of cars racing past on the highway blended with those of the nocturnal insects around him. He found himself moving to the steel fence that enclosed the campus. When he reached it, he collapsed onto the dirt, leaning his exhausted body against the barrier to support himself in a semi-seated position.

Then he started whispering. "Is this what we had agreed to, Habiba? What's going on? I don't understand you anymore! We agreed to exchange pleasure and keep me safe from any danger, and everything was going fine. But then things started moving in strange directions and getting dangerous!"

He waited several moments for her to respond but heard only cars and insects, further aggravating his anxiety.

"Habiba? Are you listening to me?"

The response began as a violent desire to scratch the skin under his chin, so he did so without hesitation. He started slowly, then scratched harder and faster until the skin became irritated ...

Yusuf flinched when he heard the sound of a cat meowing beside him, and simultaneously, his skin irritation completely stopped. He turned to his right and saw the black cat, which blended with the darkness of the night. Its eyes shining with reflected light, the animal was gazing up at him steadily and confidently.

"I hear you, as I always do."

Habiba's stern voice poured directly into his mind, but he kept his eyes on the cat, feeling goose-bumps all over as he spoke. "Why are you controlling my body and forcing me to do crazy things? Sometimes I find myself naked under the bed, and most recently inside the wardrobe! God knows where I'll find myself next time! I may wake up in the toilets because of you!"

The cat wandered around him and the sound of Habiba's hiss-like voice resonated inside his head:

"I love dark places, I love seeing your body that way, and that's the agreement."

"And what about attacking others? You did not hesitate to seriously injure Omar, and you tried to attack Yaser. Why?"

"I told you before: what hurts you hurts me, and what bothers you bothers me. This is the principle of the merging between your body and mine, and I won't allow anyone to force me out of your body. Do you understand?"

"But I can't go on living this way, Habiba!"

"And I cannot leave you, human. My presence inside your body has granted me a new and different life. I won't let anyone push me out."

"Don't hurt Yaser, Habiba. I won't tolerate anything bad happening to my best friend!"

She answered with clear annoyance, "There are things standing between me and that wretched human being, things you would not understand."

Yusuf smiled in relief when he heard her admit that, saying, "Really? Thank God."

His relief soon turned to worry and horror, however, at what she said next.

"But there are others on whom I can take revenge, so that is what I will do."

Before he could respond, the cat ran off and was swallowed by the darkness.

Chapter 78

It was after two o'clock in the morning by the time Yusuf got back to the room, and he was in a miserable state. His eyes were puffy from lack of sleep, his hair and clothes were caked with dirt, and his whole body ached, especially his legs.

He had no idea how Yaser would greet him after everything he had told him and, especially, after Habiba's fearsome display of aggression. Yusuf was reluctant to go back, but there was no choice but to face the music from his friend.

As soon as he entered the room and saw Yaser, sadness gripped his heart because his friend was sleeping in a chair, sitting upright opposite the door: it was as though he were awaiting Yusuf's return despite what must have been profound and well-founded fears. He resisted a powerful urge to cry out to his friend, deciding to wake him as gently and quietly as possible.

Yaser woke in a panic nonetheless, instinctively shouting and trying to escape, but Yusuf held his arm firmly, saying, "No, Yaser, it's okay. Don't freak out. It's really me, Yusuf. Don't worry, that demon's not here."

Yaser's curiosity overcame his fear, and he calmed down at once. He examined Yusuf closely, trying to do a deep dive into his eyes to make sure it was really him, then asked, "She's not here? How would you know? We can't see her!"

"Trust me, Yaser. The physical and spiritual merging between me and her is so strong that I can tell whether she's inside me or not, and besides: she admitted that she can't hurt you."

Yaser was understandably relieved to hear that, exclaiming "Really?! She said that? Thanks to God, thanks to God."

He took a deep breath and let it out slowly, releasing some of his stress and pent-up emotions. Then something occurred to him, so he asked,

"But if Habiba isn't inside you, where is she? And what made her leave you?"

Yusuf frowned and sighed, then shared the bitter truth: "Unfortunately, she may be attacking another person even as we speak. When she left me, the last thing she said was that she was going to retaliate against someone else."

Yaser put a hand on his head and uttered a brief prayer before asking, "Who's the victim? Do you know? Maybe we can warn them!"

Yusuf felt all the strength drain out of his body. He shook his head right and left, then murmured, "That's what tortures me, Yaser. I don't know!"

"Have you had any kind of argument or disagreement with anyone recently? Anyone insult you? Anything like that? Please, try to remember."

Yusuf shook his head again, saying: "I wracked my mind thinking about that the whole time I was coming back here, and I came up blank. I can't think of anyone who's done or said anything that would give her a reason to target them."

"So where did she go?"

Yusuf raised his eyes to the ceiling in prayer. "Oh, God, have mercy on us and have mercy on whoever is facing that demon now."

Chapter 79

"That sounds devilishly fun!" Noha laughed into the mouthpiece of her phone as she chatted with her friend Nawal. The latter had just told her about the adventure she was planning with her boyfriend after all the exams were over, and that gave Noha an idea.

"I should plan something similar with Yusuf and ... "

She gasped and turned to look at the spot where the sudden noise had come from. It sounded like a knock. Just one, and fairly strong. Unexpected, out of nowhere, and tight there on her bedroom window!

"What's wrong, Noha? Are you still there?"

Noha kept staring at the window and answered slowly, "Yes ... I'm still here."

"What's up?"

"I heard a strange sound coming from the window. It was like something heavy bumped into it from the outside."

"Your window? Are you sure? Could it have come from the street?"

"Maybe, but ... "

She cut herself off again, and a feeling of anxiety rose into her throat. This time there were two knocks spaced several seconds apart. Slow, deliberate, and definitely on the window. Now there could be no doubt: someone was knocking on the thick glass.

She told Nawal, who answered, "At two o'clock in the

morning?! Who could be knocking on your window? And why?"

"There is one crazy possibility," Noha admitted. "It might be Yusuf."

"Yusuf?! Impossible! How? That's nuts!"

"I'm not saying it was him. I don't know yet. But like I told you before, I did give him the address of our house. The question is whether he would be daring enough to come without telling me in advance."

Now the knocks returned, this time more insistently, and Noha said, "I have to open the window and see who it is."

"But what if it's not Yusuf?"

Noha's voice faltered from nervousness: "It has to be him, Nawal. It can't be anyone else. Oh my God. I'm not ready for such a sudden meeting!"

"Okay I'll leave you to it. Take care, my friend, and don't go too far with him. Goodbye."

"Goodbye, Nawal."

Noha put the handset back in its cradle and got up to comb her hair in front of the mirror. Then she gathered her courage and moved slowly towards the window, each knock intensifying her anxiety. She blamed herself for the situation because it was she who had told him her address despite her misgivings. That was why he was being so reckless now by coming to her home, putting them both in a very compromising position despite his earlier assurances that he only wanted to know it so he could picture the distance between their hearts.

The house had only a ground floor, so the glass was frosted to keep anybody from seeing inside, but the corollary to that was that if you wanted look outside, you had to open the window. She held the knob with a trembling hand and pulled in a deep breath, trying to calm herself down. Then she turned the knob to pull the moving parts inwards and peered through the opening.

No one!

Annoyed, she opened the window wider and stuck her head out, looking all over for Yusuf, but the courtyard was empty and very quiet. Now she was very much at a loss. She kept looking around, wondering if she had misinterpreted the events of the past few minutes. She did a quick mental review: first there had been a single knock on the window, then a pair, then a whole series, and now there was no one in the courtyard. *So who was knocking on the window?*

"In the name of God, the Most Gracious and the Most Merciful, what is going on?" she murmured. Her confusion was turning to worry, and a cold breeze was playing with her hair, making her shiver, so she did a quick final scan before closing the window and going back to the ...

Noha might have screamed, but a massive and involuntary inhalation stopped her cold, and by the time she was able to breathe again, she uttered a soft prayer instead: "I seek refuge in God from Satan."

A black cat stood confidently in the middle of her room, staring up at her defiantly. She wondered how on earth the animal had managed to get inside her room with the door closed.

Noha looked a little more closely and could have sworn the cat wore a sinister smile, but before she could reproach herself for an overactive imagination, she witnessed something even less likely but far more terrifying. As she watched in disbelief, the cat transformed into an unusually tall woman with dark skin and wavy hair as red as fire. She wore an unearthly black dress.

And then she started walking towards Noha, slowly but

menacingly. Noha panicked and made a hasty retreat, but soon she reached the wall behind her. Searching for a way out and finding none, her eyes went back to the fiery-haired woman in the black dress. Then the woman spoke, her voice angry and contemptuous.

"You are the girl whom Yusuf loved without even seeing?" Habiba hissed. " How foolish he is! You cannot give him a quarter of what I can."

Noha was too horrified to make sense of what she was hearing. She was losing control of her muscles, and her central nervous system was on the brink of collapse. She was dimly aware that she was about to wet herself but powerless to prevent it, and just when she thought she would faint, the angry woman transformed again, this time into a cloud of black smoke that attacked a particular spot in the girl's head. Noha cried out in agony, and darkness closed in from all sides.

Chapter 80

The following few days were the most challenging for Yusuf and Yaser since their arrival in Eastern Province. In addition to the usual anxiety and exhaustion that afflicts most students during final exams, they also had good reason to worry about their safety. On top of all that, the two young men worried about which "others" could be targets for the "revenge" that Habiba had threatened to inflict.

It was the evening before the last day of exams, and Yaser seemed even gloomier than during the previous few days. When Yusuf inquired about the reason for his mood, Yaser asked him, "Have you had any phone conversations with Noha since the exams started?"

The question was both surprising and confusing to Yusuf.

"Noha?" he said. "What could she have to do with what's troubling you today?"

"Please answer me. Have you called her?"

"I called her house a few times but got no answer. But tell me, Yaser, why are you asking about her? Does she have anything to do with what's bothering you?"

Yaser closed his eyes and covered them with his hands, saying, "No might nor power but in God."

Yusuf rose from his chair and went to sit beside his friend on the bed. He grabbed his shoulder and said, "What's the matter? Please, talk to me. My nerves can't handle the suspense."

Yaser finally opened his eyes but avoided looking at Yusuf's when he spoke. "I overheard some students talking, and one of them said his girlfriend had passed on information she heard about something weird that happened to one of the random dating girls. He didn't mention any names, but I'm afraid they were talking about Noha."

Yusuf's heart rate started to accelerate, but he tried to rule out the possibility.

"That's impossible, Yaser!" he said. "Noha never caused me any kind of distress or pain. No, she could not be the targeted person, no way!"

"I expected that kind of denial from you, and I understand it, but the details about the incident made it seem like the victim might well be her. Maybe the demon just decided to attack another category of the people connected to you!"

"What incident? Tell me the details."

"The story that's going around involves a jinn. The girl apparently told her family and her doctor that a black cat appeared in her room and that the cat transformed itself into a woman and attacked her."

Yusuf started to scratch the skin under its chin. He got up off the bed and took a few steps back before asking hesitantly,

"And the girl! What happened to her?!"

Yaser's features communicated mostly sadness, but his eyes were pure rage.

"God is Sufficient for us! Most Excellent is He in Whom we trust! I pray to God to take revenge on Habiba for all that she is doing," he said.

"Tell me about the girl. Is she okay?"

"She's alive, Yusuf. But no, she's not okay."

Yaser was silent for a moment. Then he told his best friend the tragic news.

Chapter 81

"No, it can't be!"

Yaser's heart broke as he took in the grief and shock in his friend's eyes.

"Yusuf, believe me, I also hope the victim isn't Noha, but everything about the description of the attack leads to the same suspect: that demon, Habiba."

Yusuf could feel Habiba's presence inside his body, so he backed away from Yaser, closed his eyes, and said out loud: "Habiba, tell me you haven't blinded anyone, or if you have, tell me it was someone else, not Noha. Please!"

Hearing only silence, he waited a little bit and then called out again.

"Habiba! I know you're inside me right now. I can feel it, so please answer me. Tell me the truth. Tell me you haven't cut the last cord joining me to you."

Yaser's whole body stiffened as he listened to Yusuf summoning the demon. He could not help but to recall what happened the last time, when Habiba had tried to turn Yusuf into a weapon aimed right at him. Nonetheless, he steeled himself, rose up from his bed, and took a few steps towards his oldest friend, saying,

"Nothing joins you to her, man. It's nothing more than a void agreement with no clear terms, and God willing, you will be rid of her soon."

As soon as Yaser finished, Yusuf's features were suddenly

transformed into a mask of cruelty and darkness. Then his lips moved, but it was Habiba's sharp, slithery voice that came out.

"Shut up, wretched human!" she hissed. "I wish I could pull your tongue from your mouth!"

Yaser could feel the hair stand up on the back of his neck and retreated instinctively, but then he remembered that something prevented her from harming him. *Or at least that's what she told Yusuf,* he thought to himself. Despite his trepidation, he decided to run the risk, so he willed himself to stand his ground and folded his arms across his chest, striking a defiant pose.

"If you can pull my tongue, do it, cursed demon! I'm right here, standing in front of you. Come on, what are you waiting for?!"

He was quite sure that she was more than capable of hurting him, but he put all his trust in God despite having no idea what it was that prevented her from attacking him.

Habiba unleashed an enraged roar from Yusuf's mouth and forced his body forward. Yusuf's feet moved the rest of him towards Yaser with nerve-wracking sluggishness, like a slow-motion replay during a sportscast. Then Habiba spoke again, her voice livid with hate:

"That foolish human was such easy prey! I took her eyesight to prevent her from seeing Yusuf's body because it belongs only to me!"

Yaser tried to hold his nerve, but he feared that Yusuf may have been mistaken about the demon's inability to harm him, so he backed up a little to maintain a safe distance. He was getting near the bed, though, just like the last time, so he held fast and braced himself, muttering,

"Come on, Yusuf! Do something, for God's sake!"

Yusuf's body had got to within a single step of Yaser's when the former's face suddenly changed. While the features still reflected rage, now it was a righteous one fuelled by empathy. Tears flowed from Yusuf's eyes, but he was winning the battle, and when he regained the power to speak, his voice was strong.

"I heard your filthy confession," he said. "God curse you, Habiba! Noha did nothing wrong, showing only interest in me and care for my feelings. I'm fed up with seeing you hurt people around me, do you understand? I won't put up with it anymore!"

Yaser rushed to the door and locked it to make sure Yusuf could not run away again. He also resolved to block the exit with own body, so he put his back to the door, turning to see how his friend's confrontation with the demon was going.

What he saw shook him to his very core.

Chapter 82

Yusuf wished Habiba had a physical body that could be made to materialize in front of him; then he could punch her in the face in a way that released the guilt and remorse he felt for all the people who had suffered because of his poor decisions. The lab supervisor, the security guard, his hall-mate Omar, and now the adorable and innocent Noha! Who might be next? No *more*, he thought. He had had enough of her hate and duplicity, but also of his own self-reproach. *As Yaser said, God is Sufficient for us! Most Excellent is He in Whom we trust!*

He could not let her keep preying on anyone else, but that was easier said than done. Then he had a crazy idea that came from something the demon herself had told him more than once: *"What hurts you hurts me."*

He said in a triumphant tone, "That's exactly what I'm going to do, Habiba. I will cause you pain by hurting myself."

Then he started to hit himself in the head and face as hard as he could. He threw punches, karate chops, and palm strikes, using both hands and ignoring the damage to his own body in a vicious self-inflicted assault.

Yaser's mind could not believe what his eyes were seeing. *It's like a bad film about the craziest inmate at a psychiatric hospital,* he thought.

"Yusuf, stop!" he cried.

But Yusuf continued, bashing himself with blow after blow

between fragments of the same sentence he kept repeating:

"I won't stop ... Nothing will ... ease my ... guilt ... but giving that demon ... a taste of pain!"

"Not this way, please, stop."

Yusuf could feel lumps and bruises rising, making each blow more painful than the last, but still he continued the beating. Yaser finally went to him and grabbed him by both arms, but his friend would not be denied: Yusuf pushed him down with surprising strength before running violently into the wall and then collapsing. He stayed on the floor for several moments, moaning in pain.

"Yusuf, this is insane! Stop what you're doing or you'll never recover!"

Yusuf's head came off the floor with a look of savage fury and malice. Habiba's spiteful voice came out from between his swollen lips:

"How cunning you are, Yusuf! I did not foresee you doing this, but if you want pain, I will give you some."

Yaser's head throbbed from the madness he was witnessing, and he regretted having told his friend what he had heard about Noha. But there was no time for remorse now. He saw with horror how Habiba was controlling his friend's body. She forced him to stand up, walk to the wardrobe, and ram his own head against its heavy door, brutally and repeatedly. Yusuf's moans took on a delirious tone.

Yaser had no idea how to stop what was happening, but nor had he given up. He jumped to his feet and shouted, "No God but God! God have mercy on us!"

Suddenly Yusuf walked away from the wardrobe, his facial expression indicating that he was still under the demon's control. She walked him haltingly to the shelves attached to

ROOM NUMBER 8

the wall, and he grabbed something from the middle shelf. Something that made his face smile fiercely.

The same object filled Yaser with dread. His eyes widened in horror and he could hear the blood pumping through his veins.

"Noooo!!"

Chapter 83

Now Yaser felt truly helpless. With Habiba inside it, Yusuf's body was far too strong for him to overpower, and whilst he otherwise might have hoped for intervention by other residents, it was the night before the last day of exams: everyone was out, taking advantage of dedicated study venues on campus that offered peace and quiet and all the reference materials they might need. The fact that no had come to the room thus far – despite the unholy racket taking place – only confirmed his fears. No one was coming to the rescue.

He kept screaming at Yusuf to put the knife down, but it was the demon who controlled his body, and when her voice came out of his mouth again, any doubt about her intentions evaporated.

"And now, Yusuf," she said malevolently, "how about experiencing the pain caused by cutting your skin with this sharp blade?"

Yaser's heart burned with despair. The end-game was upon them, and he could do nothing to change the outcome. Yusuf's face and head were already a mass of bruises and abrasions, and now this evil demon was about to make him turn a knife on himself. He was on the point of giving up when he heard Yusuf's real voice – not in the here and now, but rather in his mind as he recalled their last confrontation with this abomination: "No, Habiba, my friend Yaser is a red line I would never let you cross!"

Almost unconsciously, Yaser knew what to do, shouting:

"My friend Yusuf is a red line, demon!"

He also put his words into action, he rushing to where his friend was standing and, before the latter could react, pushing him back towards the door of the wardrobe. Then Yaser went all in: he enveloped Yusuf in a tight embrace, shielding the front of the latter's body with his own whilst pinning his back against the wardrobe.

"And now, cursed demon, if you want to cut the skin of my friend, you have to cut mine first!" he shouted.

It was a risky plan, to say the least, relying as it did on the assumption that Habiba really could not hurt him. Initially, the gambit appeared to have gained some time, at least, as the demon seemed surprised by what had transpired and made no response.

Within seconds, however, she was back to her angry, aggressive self. "I have no more patience for your standing against me, wretched human!" she hissed through Yusuf's mouth. "The time has come for you to die."

Yaser felt Yusuf's arm raise the knife into the air. There was no way he could stop it, not without exposing Yusuf's vital organs to mortal injury if that was what the demon had in mind. Instead, he closed his eyes and readied himself for death.

Habiba remained in control of Yusuf's body, but his friend's repeated interference in her plans had infuriated her. She brought the arm down hard, directing the sharp blade towards her new prey ...

Yaser.

Chapter 84

Yaser felt the downward movement of his friend's arm and heard the sounds of the blade slicing through the air and then penetrating something. He waited for the pain to register. When it did not, he opened his eyes and saw Yusuf's arm alongside him, his hand still clutching the handle of the knife, the point of whose blade was right next to the back of his knee, several centimetres deep in the thick wood of the wardrobe door.

When Yaser raised his eyes to Yusuf's face, he saw a very human mix of calmness, exhaustion, and gratitude, as well as a smile that was trying but failing to hide considerable pain. Worryingly, however, Yusuf was also scratching under his chin.

Yaser still had his arms wrapped around his friend and did not let him go. His eyes scanned the room obsessively and he whispered, "Did ... ?"

Yusuf nodded his head and said in a weak voice, "Yes, old friend. We won the battle. But the war is still on."

"Is she still inside you now?

Yusuf stopped scratching before he answered,

"She just got out, but she left a parting message."

"Oh yeah? What was it?"

"She said, 'Rest assured that I will be coming back.'"

"May God condemn her."

Yaser stepped back a bit after mumbling that prayer, but

Yusuf started to collapse, so he quickly returned to his side and held him up.

"Oh, my God," Yusuf said. "You're in rough shape after going through all that. I'll take you to the clinic – right now."

Yusuf rejected the idea, insisting, "No, I'm not going anywhere. Just help me reach my bed. I need some rest, and tomorrow morning, I'll be totally fine."

Yusuf let out several moans of pain as he slowly walked to his bed with his friend supporting him. He lay on his back as Yaser got some ice cubes from their little fridge, putting some in a dish and several more in a plastic bag. Then he went back to Yusuf, sat next on the bed next to him, and started gently pressing the bag of ice cubes against his friend's bruises.

"Wow!" Yusuf exclaimed. A mischievous smile, then: "That's colder than Hell."

They both chuckled a bit at that, but the release of tension quickly upped the ante, and they laughed heartily until Yusuf started coughing. Yaser waited until his friend had caught his breath then said,

"Thank God we survived that demon. There were a few moments there when I thought we were goners."

Yusuf reached out and patted his friend on the knee, saying, "You went too far in risking yourself to protect me, Yaser. I don't know how to thank you, but you really deserve to be my best friend."

Yaser was so touched by his friend's appreciation that tears welled up in his eyes. He wiped them away with a tissue before answering: "I wouldn't deserve to be your best friend if I hadn't done what I did. But tell me, have you managed to figure out why Habiba can't directly harm me?"

"Not yet. Maybe there's some kind of spiritual bond between us that developed over long years of true friendship."

"That might be the reason, but I still blame you for all of this."

"You have every right. I never should've have hidden what I was going through from you."

"Exactly. If you had revealed was happening right from the beginning, we might have prevented all the harm that demon caused, and those people wouldn't have been hurt.

Yusuf let out a deep sigh as he looked at the ceiling.

"I know, Yaser, and it tortures me!" he said. "I was a bomb that exploded in their faces, and that feeling hurts my conscience much more than all these bruises hurt my body, but unfortunately, I was impulsive and reckless because I was seduced by the pleasant things I experienced with Habiba. I wish I could make it up to them and compensate them for the suffering I caused, but I can't, especially with Noha. How can I make her regain her sight? How?"

Yusuf burst into tears when he reached the part about Noha, and Yaser let him cry, hoping he could release some of his guilt and sadness. Yaser spoke through his own tears, saying:

"Maybe you can repair the damage Habiba has caused, but you've got a tough mission ahead of you ... Get rid of her once and for all, and stop her from hurting anyone else because of you."

He stopped for a moment, then added,

"And may God help you succeed!"

Chapter 85

The following afternoon, they were making slow progress as they packed their bags. The previous night had been dreadful. Yusuf had developed a fever, so Yaser stayed up most of the night, trying to lower his temperature with cold packs. He gave him some painkillers, too, as well as some antibiotics in case any of his wounds were infected.

Thanks to God's mercy and Yaser's ministrations, Yusuf had regained most of his strength by morning, but he could not get rid of the headache that refused to part with him. The two young men had sat for their semester finals earlier in the day, and they were both extremely worried about the results because the ordeal with Habiba had prevented them from getting in enough study time.

Yusuf also had a hard time explaining the bruises and scratches on his head and face. Just about everyone had asked, and he wasn't sure how convincing it was, but he had made up a story and was trying to stick to it.

There had been nothing new from Habiba since she had left his body the previous day. He felt neither her presence inside him, nor the urge to scratch his chin, but he was under no illusions: he knew she would be back.

They were still packing when the telephone rang in their hall, and one of the students from down the corridor hollered that he would answer. Yusuf refocused on his luggage until he heard somebody knocking on the door of his room. He opened to find the round face of Zuhair.

"Hi, Zuhair. How are you?"

"Very well, thanks. The call's for you, my friend."

"Thanks boss. Maybe someone from my family in Makkah," Yusuf said as he got up. "I'm heading back there today."

The two students walked side by side and chatted until they reached the end of the corridor, where Zuhair returned to his room, whilst Yusuf walked towards the telephone. He picked up the handset and said, "Hello?"

"Hello, Yusuf."

A storm of contradicting emotions swept over Yusuf as soon as he heard the voice. He felt surprise and joy, but also anxiety and awkwardness.

"Noha!"

Her voice was laden with grief and sarcasm.

"Yes, I'm Noha the blind!"

Yusuf had no words for such a moment, and who could blame him? What do you say to a woman for whose blindness you are indirectly responsible?

But he tried, his voice trembling and stuttering.

"I truly cannot find the words ... for such an ... absurdly unjust situation," he said. "I pray for God to help you, and I sincerely apologize ... for what that cursed demon did to you."

She did not reply at once, and he realized that she was crying. He gave her all the time she needed to steady herself. Finally she spoke again, shakily.

"Apologizing will not restore the light to my eyes, but I'm waiting for you to tell me the whole story of her," Noha said. "Now."

Yusuf was unprepared for this, but if anyone deserved the truth, it was Noha. So he lowered his voice and recounted the main incidents in his story with Habiba. When he finished, Noha cried again for some time. Then she said, "No God but God. Why didn't you tell me about all that from the beginning?"

"Noha, how can anyone know what they should hide and what they should share with others? It's not always easy to define that, especially when these things are related to spiritual issues that the vast majority of people don't believe in."

He heard a deep sigh before Noha responded, "Anyway, I think what happened to me was a warning from God that I should get back on the right track."

"Yes," he agreed. "Does that mean that you've forgiven me?"

"Yusuf, you are prey, exactly like me. Your physical injuries resulting from your confrontation with Habiba last night are temporary, but I'm sure that the troubles you have because of guilt will live with you until the end of your life. Believe me, I'm not mad or resentful at you. On the contrary, I pity you for all that you have suffered – and for what you are going to suffer in the future."

Rather than relieving him, her words fell heavily on his heart. He was overwhelmed with emotions and stayed silent, so she said:

"This is the last telephone call between us, and I wanted it to be on your last day here before you travel. Although I now realize that the idea of random dating was wrong, I have to thank you for having treated me respectfully, and I hope God will destroy that demon and grant you a happy life. I also pray to God to help me cope with the dramatic change that has happened to my life."

She was trying to resist an overwhelming desire to burst into tears, but she failed, managing just a few more words interspersed with sobs and gasps:

"And now ... goodbye ... Yusuf."

His tears flowed, too, as he whispered, "Goodbye, Noha."

He put the handset down quickly and ran back to his room to avoid being seen by anyone. He wanted to do the rest of his crying in private, inside the walls of his own room. At the same time, in another place, Noha collapsed into the embrace of her friend Nawal, who had helped her make her last call to Yusuf and now shared her tears.

Chapter 86

Yaser was about to open a box containing a new portable stereo when Yusuf got back to the room and went straight to his bed. Seeing the state his friend was in, the former set the box on his desk and went to sit with him.

"Why are you crying, Yusuf?" he asked.

Yusuf told him all the details of his last call with Noha, and how it had affected not only his emotions but his entire being. Yaser nodded his head and patted his friend's shoulder in understanding, saying:

"What a wise girl! I agree with every single word she said. May God help you both with your suffering. Now come on, mate, brush off the dust of the battle and get ready for a new round. Let's finish packing our bags and head to the airport."

Yusuf took a big breath and let the air out slowly in an attempt to calm himself. Feeling a little better, he asked, "Why did you buy a new stereo today when we're travelling? You should've waited until we return for the next semester."

Yaser went to the desk and started taking the device out of its box, saying, "In normal circumstances, you'd be right, but let's do what we couldn't do before. We will let Surat Al-Baqarah fill the room, even after we leave, and because Habiba is not inside you now, she can't stop me this time."

"Fine by me," Yusuf agreed. "Without a doubt, your mum knows more than us such issues. May God protect her."

Minutes later, the warm, soothing sounds of a professional

Quran reciter flowed from the stereo. The two young men listened in silence as they finished packing their bags and changed their clothes. After they got their luggage into the corridor, they went back inside for one last look at the room.

That was when it started.

Before their eyes, the chair next to Yaser's desk turned itself upside down. Both startled, they exchanged looks of foreboding. Then some tools started flying off one of the shelves and onto the floor.

"I seek refuge in God from the cursed Satan!" Yusuf shouted whilst taking a few steps backward. "What now? What's going on?

Yaser watched in disbelief as the covers floated off his bed settled on the fridge.

"Looks like Habiba might be back!" he said.

Yusuf hurried out into the corridor, then turned around to look back, saying, "I don't feel her presence, but it might be one of her tricks. Come on Yaser, get out of there before you get hurt."

Yaser tried to move, but nothing happened, and he started screaming: "No! I can't move! I don't feel my legs! Yusuf, help me!"

Even over the sound of his own fear, Yaser could hear his heart pounding. Then, as he tried to process what was happening, the situation grew even more terrifying when he noticed someone – or something – standing in one of the corners of the room. Yaser shivered as he examined the dark complexion, the menacingly masculine features, the cruel expression, and the bizarre clothing. What really shocked him, though, was that whilst it looked like a human being, it stood no more than 50 centimetres tall.

ROOM NUMBER 8

Just what we needed, Yaser thought. *Now there's an evil elf in our room.*

Yusuf was greeted by the same sight as he came back to help his friend.

"Who ... or what in the name of God is that?!" he stammered.

Yaser answered with understandable impatience, shouting, "Not important right now! Just help me get out, please!"

Yusuf started dragging his friend towards the door, but Yaser's weight seemed to have doubled, slowing their progress to a crawl. Neither took his eyes off the elf as they beat their slow-motion retreat, so they both saw what happened next.

The freakish little creature suddenly raised its hand and made a strange gesture, and one of the drawers from Yusuf's desk was suddenly launched across the room, barely missing them as it smashed into the wall.

"The damned elf is trying to kill us!" Yaser shouted.

That seemed to aggravate their foe, whose features became even fiercer as his hands turned red and started making a series of movements. The two students looked around anxiously to see what object might fly at them next.

Suddenly, the fridge started to vibrate, and because the covers of Yaser's bed had fallen on top of it, it looked like a cartoonish ghost, shaking with rage as it waited for the right moment to attack them.

Now they were really afraid. The fridge was directly across from them on the opposite wall, and its weight meant that if it hit them at anything like the speed the drawer had had, they were finished.

Still vibrating, the appliance moved slowly forward until its power cord was pulled out of the socket behind it. Then it accelerated, driven by the unseen force that seemed to have been conjured by the elf. Still unable to move, Yaser screamed as Yusuf tried one last desperate heave to get his friend to safety, but it was not enough; the fridge was upon them.

Having given up all hope, the two students suddenly rose into the air and flew out of the room, landing in a heap on their luggage in the corridor. The refrigerator followed close behind, but the door slammed shut just in time, and the collision that followed caused a deafening crack! A few pieces of wood and metal clattered on the floor, and then it was over. The only sound to be heard was that of the stereo playing the Surat Al-Baqarah.

PART IV
THE DIFFICULT RETURN

(Makkah 1994 AD)

Chapter 87

The following afternoon, Husam called his family's home in Makkah, speaking first with his parents, followed by his youngest brother. Then it was Yusuf's turn to pick up the receiver. After they had exchanged greetings, he asked, "How are your arrangements going for the summer semester?"

Husam answered in an anxious voice. "Thanks to God, the summer course will start in a few days, he said, "but ... "

His voice tailed off as he searched for the right words. Yusuf could not help but to have noticed. Now he was curious to the point of alarm, asking, "But what?! What's up? Is everything alright?"

"As a matter of fact, Yusuf, no, everything is not alright. I was coming back to my room a little while ago and saw fire engines and an ambulance near Hall 621. There was a nasty smell in the air too, so I got closer to see what had happened. "

Husam stopped to see how Yusuf would respond, but the latter remained silent, waiting for his brother to continue, so Husam got straight to the point:

"Room Number 8 was completely burned out."

Yusuf's hand shook so much that he almost dropped the phone. Then he muttered, "No God, but God. What are you saying?"

"I understand how shocked you must be; this kind of news is hard to take, coming right out of the blue. I couldn't believe it myself at first, so I went inside to see the place with my own eyes. Then I was sure it was really true."

"So my room was burned out. Do you know how it happened?"

"Preliminary investigations say it was a short circuit, possibly in some device that was still turned on when you and Yaser left. But it's difficult to confirm because there's so little evidence. The fire burned everything in the room to ashes."

"No strength but in God," Yusuf replied. "So you saw the room from the inside?"

"Yes, I did, and unfortunately, it was in very bad condition. Black soot covered everything, the furniture and the tools were all incinerated, so there was really nothing left. Even the ceiling was gone, and the smell was unbearable!"

Yusuf exhaled slowly, trying to lease the stress he felt. "What about the rest of the rooms? Was anyone hurt?"

"Luckily, the fire was just in your room, and the adjacent rooms were untouched. And as you know, the summer holiday has just started, so there very few students in the hall."

Yusuf thought a bit, then asked, "Does this mean that my desktop computer, my clothes, the novels, and all our personal belongings went up in smoke?"

Husam's voice reflected his sympathy as he answered:

"I'm afraid so. I pray God will compensate you, my brother. My thoughts are with you and Yaser. As for the room, the maintenance people say they'll have it ready for you in time for the new semester."

"Assuming Yaser and I return," Yusuf said. "Anyway, thank you very much for explaining what happened, and God bless you."

Husam wondered what, exactly, his brother meant about possibly not returning, but he figured the kid had had more than enough stress for one day, so he did not press the matter.

Chapter 88

Late at night a few days later, Yusuf felt thirsty, so he left his room and walked down the dimly lit corridor to the kitchen. He opened the refrigerator and reached in to get a small bottle of water.

That's when he noticed it, and the sight of it froze him in place.

The light from the fridge showed that his outstretched arm was covered with dark red spots and sores filled with pus! He did not believe his eyes, for his skin had been normal just a few minutes ago, and there was no way it could have changed so much so quickly. What made things worse was that the spots were itchy, making him feel compelled to scratch.

"Habiba! Was it you who did that to my arm?"

He got no response, so he closed the fridge, left his water on a table, and walked through the sitting room, heading for the toilet. He gasped as he stumbled into something on the floor, lost his balance and almost fell, but he managed to stay on his feet by putting his hand on the wall for support.

The semi-darkness did not allow him to see what he had tripped over, so he switched on the light. It took a few seconds for his eyes to adjust, and when they did, he screamed at the top of his lungs, for there on floor, face-down and motionless, lay his beloved mother!

"Mother! What's wrong with you? Answer me Mama, please!"

He kept screaming as he slapped his mother's hands, and when there was no response, he had nightmarish thoughts about what might have happened to her. He held her by the shoulder to turn her over and ...

His eyes widened and his heart pounded in his chest when he saw that her face was covered with blood!

"Oh, heavens!" he said with great difficulty. He moved her head from side to side a bit before making the horrifying discovery that her tongue was missing!

Yusuf was drowning in despair. He did not know whether his mother was already dead or if she had just lost consciousness because of pain and blood loss. He cradled her head in his arms and wept as never before, his tears flowing as though from a fountain.

Several minutes passed before another realization renewed his panic: his cries and wails over his stricken mother had been enough to wake the dead, so why had his father and his younger brother not woken up and come running?

"God curse you, demon, if this is your doing," he muttered as he gently lay his mother's head back on the carpet. He stood up slowly and walked shakily towards his parents' room, his fears redoubled when he saw the door slightly ajar. He pushed it open with trembling fingers and called,

"Father! Are you here?"

He flipped the light switch and held his head in his hands when he saw what had befallen his father, screaming:

"Noooo!!"

Alongside the echo of his own tortured scream, he also heard the gentle voice of his father wending its way into his mind:

"In the name of God, the Most Gracious and the Most Compassionate. Wake up, my son! You're having a nightmare!"

Yusuf opened his eyes and struggled to breathe as he sat upright in his bed. He was gripped by panic due to the dreadfully disturbing dream. His mother rubbed his shoulder saying,

"Calm down, my son, and say 'I seek refuge in God from Satan.' The nightmare was over when you woke up."

Relief washed over him at seeing his parents well and healthy, and he was thrilled when he saw that his mother was cuddling his little brother. He looked at all of them once more before the exhaustion caught up with him and he let his upper body fall back onto the mattress, whispering,

"Thank God you are all well. Thank you."

Then he remembered something, and quickly raised his arm in front of his face to check for the spots. He sighed in relief, but only briefly as he felt the irresistible itch on that familiar patch of skin.

Under his chin!

He had only begun to absorb what that could mean when Habiba's unyielding voice poured into his mind:

"Tell them to leave the room immediately. You have experienced how much harm I can cause them!"

Yusuf felt a quick shiver when he realized that Habiba was back inside him and could reassume control over his body. But quickly restored his calm and composure, waved his hand at his parents, and said, "Thank you, I'm fine now, please go back to sleep."

His mother and father exchanged a quick look but then left the room, bringing their youngest child with them.

Silence reigned in Yusuf's room for a few seconds. Then he asked,

"Now what, Habiba?"

She used the softest and the most alluring tones whilst answering, "Yusuf, my baby, never treat me crazily as you did in that doomed, wretched room with your wretched friend!"

Yusuf let his body relax completely, stretching his arms out and parting his legs until he was spread-eagled on the bed.

"Don't worry," he said very calmly. "I won't treat you in a crazy way."

A mysterious smile crossing his lips, he added, "Indeed, I won't be able to do anything to you or to myself."

"I do not understand what you mean!"

"You will understand everything right now."

As soon as Yusuf spoke those words, his parents dashed back into the room carrying several lengths of thick nylon rope. Without hesitation, each of them tied one of their son's hands to the nearest corner of the bed, then did the same with his feet. When they finished, Yusuf was tightly secured to all four corners of his bed. Habiba shouted madly inside his mind:

"What is this mess?!"

Yusuf laughed at her confusion and answered, "The last thing you can call this is mess, demon! Did you really believe that I would just sit around and wait for you to occupy my body again without a plan?"

"A plan? Why would you need a plan?"

"I need it to regain the freedom to make my own choices in life."

He looked at his parents and said with love, "And most importantly, to preserve the safety of the people around me, for I won't tolerate the existence of that time bomb inside me for one more second."

He felt her moving around between his internal organs like a caged lion. That caused him some pain, but he was prepared for that.

He heard her voice again inside his head. "And I will not let go of my new life, the pleasure and passion I have experienced in your body," she warned. "You cannot change that. It is your destiny."

"At least I can try, Habiba. And now I know your weak point."

"Nonsense! Your knowledge is strictly limited to humans. Don't pretend otherwise."

"Why do you think I'm all tied up?"

The demon seemed to have no answer for that.

"I will tell you," Yusuf said. "I asked my father and mother to tie me down this way to stop me from scratching the skin under my chin. Forcing me to scratch is the only way you can get out of my body when you decide to attack others. If we prevent the scratching, you will remain imprisoned inside me."

His mother rubbed her hands in tension as she followed his side of the conversation without being able to hear the evil spirit inside him.

Habiba giggled in a way that made Yusuf's head throb, then said,

"What do you gain by keeping me inside your body? You won't be trapped this way forever. I will get out as soon as you can no longer tolerate the ropes."

Despite the pain in his head and other parts of his body, Yusuf laughed, too.

Then he said, "You may possess great powers, demon, but our weapon now is much more powerful than you. Now you will understand what I gain by locking you up inside me."

Yusuf's parents knew this last statement was the cue for their next part in the plan. Days earlier, they had consulted with a learned sheikh specialized in using the Holy Quran to heal people who suffered from various ailments – including possession by *jinn*, or demons. He had advised them on which Quranic verses were most effective at tormenting and expelling evil spirits, and now they put their training to good use, taking turns reciting the passages they had memorized.

Sure enough, the sound of these verses drove Habiba into a frenzy as she finally understood the threat posed by Yusuf's plan. She did everything in her considerable power to free one of his arms and force him to scratch, which in turn would allow her to leave his body and attack his parents. She willed one of Yusuf's arms to strain and flail mightily, inflicting hideous scratches and friction burns on his skin, but whilst he suffered severe pain, the specially selected rope held firm. Then she tried the other arm and got the same result.

With each passing moment, Habiba was suffering her own pain and torment due to the holy verses Yusuf's parents kept reciting. Now she went to work on them, using Yusuf's tongue to address them directly. The cunning demon alternated between bloodcurdling threats and pathetic pleading that shocked the couple, but it was no use. Both Yusuf's plan and the guidance of the healer dictated that no matter how bad things got, there must be no retreat, no wavering, no tolerance that would grant any sort of opening or respite to the evil spirit.

And they stuck to the plan.

After about two hours of torturing Yusuf's body and testing his parents' nerves and tempers, it was Habiba who broke.

"Damn you all!!" she screamed through Yusuf's mouth. "I call the kings of the jinn to curse you!!"

There followed an unholy, ear-piercing shriek. And then nothing.

Yusuf's body convulsed a couple of times, his mouth opening wide and his throat expanding as if he were about to vomit. His eyes bulged sickeningly as he gazed up at the ceiling in a way that broke his parents' hearts because it could only mean their son was suffering. Both of them recoiled in horror as what appeared to be black smoke coming out of his mouth, but it soon dissipated. Once it was gone, Yusuf's body relaxed completely, and he closed his eyes in exhaustion.

At that moment, the couple realized that they had won the war for his soul, that thanks to God, Habiba would no longer be able to control Yusuf's body. She had been expelled by the power of the Holy Quran. His mother burst into tears, whilst his father bowed down in prostration to thank God for His blessing.

Only later did they understand just how costly the victory had been, for Habiba had enacted a final toll of revenge before being forced out of Yusuf's body.

The demon had lost the war, but she had taken something whose absence would remind them and their son of her forever.

She had taken his voice.

The End

Epilogue
(Riyadh 2002 AD)

When Amal finished reading the novel "Room Number 8", tears flooded her eyes and ran down her cheeks. She was struggling to resist the urge to cry aloud, so her husband turned to her and wiped some of her tears away with his fingers.

Then he said tenderly, "No, my dear, hold on, don't cry. Yusuf and I are both fine, as you know."

She pulled a tissue from the box beside her, soaking up more tears and drying her nose before replying in a choked voice,

"Thank God you're safe after all those dreadful events, but poor Yusuf suffered so much, physically and psychologically, from his connection with Habiba until he managed to get rid of her."

"Yes, that's right. Thank God for everything."

"But even after all that suffering, that cursed demon robbed him of his ability to speak when she eventually left his body."

Yaser nodded his head in agreement, his facial expression indicating distress as he recalled those memories.

"That was very sad indeed, and as I've told you before, Yusuf went through various medical tests to diagnose the damage to his vocal cords, and he also had a long treatment journey, moving between different hospitals here in Saudi Arabia and in the USA. There has been some progress, but he still needs more time and many more prayers from all of us."

"I pray to God to heal him."

Yaser pointed at the novel his wife was holding and added,

"It was during his stay in the USA that he decided to vent his internal distress by recording his suppressed memories on paper. Then he sent the manuscript to me and asked me to help find a publishing company that would publish his story and distribute the book. And now here it is in the hands of readers, and you're one of the first people to read it."

Amal rose and moved towards the packing boxes in the corner of the sitting room. She and her husband were moving to a new house the following day. She placed the book in one of the boxes, then sighed and said,

"A very impressive novel. Anyway, we have to finish closing the rest of the boxes. It's getting late."

Yaser got up to give her a helping hand whilst murmuring, "God help us."

The next evening, Yaser threw his exhausted body on the new bed next to his wife and let out a brief sigh that turned into a yawn. Then he said, "Moving in and arranging all the stuff was a lot of work. I'm much more tired than usual."

Amal turned onto her side to face him, smiling encouragingly and stroking his hair with her fingers.

"You're right, baby," she told him. "It was a long and exhausting day, but thanks to God, the n ew house is bigger and more beautiful than the flat we were living in."

He yawned again, muttering in a sleepy voice,

"Of course. Thank God."

His wife was no less tired than he was, but her excitement about the new house was still overcoming her exhaustion and aching muscles.

In minutes, Yaser's breathing was settling into regularity, so Amal kissed his cheek and closed her eyes to join him in the realm of sleep.

After midnight, Yaser suddenly opened his eyes. He lay on his right side, facing the wall nearest that side of the bed. The lighting was dim, as he had left it before going to sleep, but he had a strange feeling, one he had never experienced before. He felt something moving – not under his clothes, but inside his body!

He did not understand what he was feeling, but it was unpleasant, so he tried to alleviate his discomfort by changing his position ...

His muscles did not respond!

He tried to call out to Amal, but his vocal cords failed to comply!

Now he was besieged by fear and worry, and both were amplified when a sharp feminine voice was poured directly into his mind, another extraordinary occurrence that Yaser had never experienced before.

"Does what you feel now surprise you, human?"

His heart shivered and his eyes widened in disbelief. With strenuous effort, he managed to articulate a single word that left his lips as a whisper:

"Habiba?"

A devilishly naughty giggle echoed through his mind before the owner of the voice answered,

"No, I am not her. On the contrary, I am the one who prevented her – and still prevents her – from attacking you."

Yaser remembered being surprised that Habiba could not attack him directly whilst she was controlling Yusuf's body, but he had never understood why.

"Who are you?"

"I am Maika, the daughter of one of the kings of the jinn from the Moska tribe. I was watching you long ago before I had the chance to enter your body in that room. I stopped

Habiba and all t   t room from hurting you, even though you killed some of them!"

"I killed some of them?"

"Yes, the scorpion, the rat, the ants, the elf. Do you remember all that?"

A fearsome coldness swept over his body as he recalled all the incidents she referred to. It was all he could do to ask another question, his voice weak and trembling.

"Why do you protect me?"

Maika was silent for some time, further heightening Yaser's stress and fear, before she answered,

"Because you are a different person ... Rare ... You have many traits that others do not have, so I want you for myself. I will be your wife. Do you understand me?"

Her words only increased his fear and confusion at what was happening, and he knew only part of it. His eyes felt normal, for instance, but if he could have seen them at that moment, he would have noticed the dark redness that had come into them. His mind let out a scream. Had that scream escaped his lips, its echoes would have filled the whole house ...

House Number 888.

Closing Whisper

Dear Readers,

Since I started writing novels in 2008 AD, I have been delighted to receive your impressions and inquiries through various communication channels, including emails, forums, and social media applications. I urge you to sustain this effective interaction, through which we can activate the three elements of what I call the "Triangle of Success for Books," which consist of the author, the readers, and the publisher.

However, since all of my publications depend on suspense, mystery, and surprise, so I beg your pardon to ask a favour: whether you are posting on my account or yours, please only offer general impressions of my works lest we spoil the pleasure of reading for those who have not had the chance to read them yet.

If and when you want to dive deep into the details, there is always space for that through direct interaction with me instead of public messages.

I appreciate your understanding, and I will be waiting for your impressions about all my publications with all my love.

Yahya Khan

About the author:

Yahya Khan was born in Jeddah in the Kingdom of Saudi Arabia in 1975. In 1998, he received bachelor of science (Bsc) degree with honours in electrical engineering from King Fahd University of Petroleum and Minerals in Dhahran. During his time at KFUPM, he participated in writing a set of articles (in Arabic and English), in cultural periodicals issued by the College of Engineering Sciences. He also contributed articles on various topics in print and online publications, including Shams, Today, Neutrality, and Generations. On graduating, he joined the Saudi Petrochemical Company in the same year and worked in Jubail Industrial City, before moving to the Training and Development Department at SABIC Headquarters in 2014. In late 2008, he published his first novel Room No. 8, which featured a new style of writing for KSA. This was followed by a series of different publications featuring diverse topics and ideas whilst preserving the elements of suspense, mystery, and purposeful implicit messages. Khan created a questionnaire to study the reading habits of readers through various online communication channels, later publishing the resulting statistics and percentages in local newspapers. He also presented a new theory called the "Triangle of Success for Books", in which he explained a model that connects the author, the reader, and the publishing company, and highlighted the importance of strengthening the relationships among them through the application of elements of "comprehensive quality management" in literary production. This theory was published in local newspapers, and it was also discussed on the Saudi Cultural Channel and the Sabah Cultural Program. There is also a YouTube interview with the author on this subject. His interests include reading, writing, and watching football and documentaries.

Other works of fiction:
Between the Walls of the Cave (Novel 2009)
A Saudi Child in Paris (Real Diaries 2011)
When Darkness attacked (Collection of Short Stories 2011)
House Number 888 (Novel 2013)
We Want Your Eyes (Novel 2016)

To interact with the author:
Email: yak2008new@yahoo.com
Facebook: www.facebook.com/yahyak1
X: @yahyakhan2011
Instagram: yahyakhan2913
Snapchat: @yahyakhan2015

You can also take part in evaluating the publications of the author, and/or read the impressions of readers from around the Arab world, on the international reading site Goodreads at www.goodreads.com.